Malini

TITLES IN THIS SERIES

THROUGH MY EYES
series editor Lyn White

Malini

ROBERT HILLMAN

ALLEN&UNWIN
SYDNEY·MELBOURNE·AUCKLAND·LONDON

A portion of the proceeds (up to $5000) from sales of this series will be donated to UNICEF. UNICEF works in over 190 countries, including those in which books in this series are set, to promote and protect the rights of children.   www.unicef.org.au

First published in 2014
Text © Robert Hillman 2014
Series concept © series creator and series editor Lyn White 2014

Allen & Unwin
83 Alexander Street, Crows Nest NSW 2065, Australia
Phone: (61 2) 8425 0100
Email: info@allenandunwin.com
Web: www.allenandunwin.com

A Cataloguing-in-Publication entry is available from
the National Library of Australia – www.trove.nla.gov.au

ISBN 978 1 74331 255 1

Teaching and learning guide available from www.allenandunwin.com

Cover design concept by Bruno Herfst & Vincent Agostino
Cover design by Sandra Nobes
Cover photos: portrait of young girl by Gunnar Salvarsson, displacement in the Vanni by trokilinochchi/Wikimedia Commons
Text design by Bruno Herfst & Vincent Agostino
Map of Sri Lanka by Guy Holt
Set in 11pt Plantin
This book was printed in August 2016 at Griffin Press, Australia.

10 9 8 7 6 5 4 3

To the people of Sri Lanka, with humility

Chapter 1

Malini watched the Tamil Tiger commander intently.

She was standing with the other students under the six hemlocks that had been planted by the British half a century earlier.

The commander, dressed in his tiger-stripe uniform and peaked cap, had come to the school and told Malini's father, the principal, that he wished to address all of the students – twenty-two boys, one hundred and twenty-eight girls. It was a request that could not be refused: the Tiger commander was accompanied by ten armed soldiers.

'This year,' the commander said, 'the war will be won. The soldier-martyrs of the Liberation Tigers of Tamil Eelam will tear the hearts from the chests of our enemies. In fire and blood, our homeland will be born. And you will play your part.' He extended his hand towards a group of six boys standing together under one of the hemlocks, the youngest, Malini knew, just eleven years old.

'Come to me,' he said to the group of boys, then added, with an odd sort of courtesy, 'thayavuseithu, please.'

After some hesitation, the six boys walked to the front of the gathering and lined up beside the commander. He only ever took six boys at any one time.

Malini closed her eyes and offered a brief, silent prayer to Shiva. She had seen this a dozen times before.

Malini's father looked away to the left, above the trees. His face was a mask of grief. The other teachers – ten of them, standing behind him – looked at the ground to disguise their emotions. The girls among the assembled students, a few of them, uttered little cries of dismay. The boys remained impassive.

Beside the commander was a stack of automatic rifles standing upright with their stocks on the ground and the barrels resting together, like the structure of a tent. The commander took up the rifles, two at a time, and handed one to each of the boys who had come forward. The boys accepted the rifles shyly.

The commander said, 'Raise your guns.'

The boys lifted their rifles above their heads.

The commander said, 'Death to the enemies of Tamil Eelam.'

The boys murmured, 'Death to the enemies of Tamil Eelam.'

'Louder!' said the commander.

The boys cried out, 'Death to the enemies of Tamil Eelam!'

Then the commander said, 'Go back to your homes.

Say farewell to your father. Say farewell to your mother. A soldier will accompany you.'

The boys were smiling, perhaps because they thought it best to appear happy about being conscripted. Tears ran down the cheeks of the youngest boy, but he still attempted to smile.

Before the boys left, each with a soldier to watch him, Malini's father embraced them and kissed the tips of his fingers, then touched their foreheads.

Tears found a path down Malini's face. She would never see these boys again. They would fight the enemy, and they would die. Ghanan, Nalinan, Agilan, Cholla, Mihuthan, Nithi. In her heart, Malini said goodbye to each.

Malini's town of Satham lay among green fields on the eastern coast of Sri Lanka, close to where the blue waters of the Indian Ocean formed the vast Bay of Bengal. The city of Trincomalee reached out to Koddiyar Bay fifty kilometres further north, while to the south, nearer than Trincomalee, the town of Kathiraveli sat just off the highway to Batticaloa.

Satham was big enough to have both a primary school and the high school that Malini attended. At age fourteen, she was in the ninth year of her education.

Satham was a Tamil town, one of many on this part of the coast. The Tamil people made up only twelve per cent of the island's population and they sought security by keeping close. This had never been more important than in this time of civil war, when the minority Tamils and the majority Sinhalese were engaged in a fight to the death. Malini wondered if it was really true that all Tamils and all Sinhalese were enemies. Her father had told her that, for centuries, Tamils and Sinhalese had got along. It was only in the last sixty years that Tamils had felt so persecuted in their own land.

Malini knew the history of her country well. Once a Portuguese colony, then a British colony, Sri Lanka had barely known true independence in modern times up until 1948. The British soldiers marched down to the docks that year and boarded ships for England, leaving behind a nation of Tamils and Sinhalese anxious to preserve their identities in what was, in many ways, a brand new land. The new Sri Lanka was a democracy with one parliament, a vast patchwork of customs and two major religious faiths: Hinduism (the Tamil faith) and Buddhism (the Sinhalese faith). More than ever in the past, Tamils felt threatened by the majority Sinhalese. More than ever, the Sinhalese majority made the Tamil people feel as if Sri Lanka was not their home.

In the north of the island, where Tamils were in the majority, an army was formed in 1976, the LTTE: Liberation Tigers of Tamil Ealam. This new army had one aim: to create in the north and east of the island a Tamil homeland. And so in 1983, the war had begun, and the bloodshed was frightening.

Malini thought of Satham as paradise. The soil in the fields surrounding the town was so rich that people said you could throw a plum stone over your shoulder in the evening and find a fully grown tree in the morning. An exaggeration, of course, but it was true that the rice fields that stretched towards the hills in the west produced an abundant crop each year. Winds from the south-east brought in the monsoons from the Indian Ocean, filling hundreds of small streams, which in turn filled the many lakes that fed the rice fields. Even the weather was better in Malini's town than elsewhere on the eastern coast. In the hottest months of the year, from April to June, a cool breeze came off the ocean each evening and made the nights more bearable.

That afternoon, Malini collected her little sister from the primary school and they walked home together as they always did, not a long walk but a sad one. Malini told Banni about what had happened at school and Banni plagued her with questions she couldn't answer: *Would the boys who were conscripted today come home when the war was over? What would happen to their schooling? Would they still practise maths and history and all those things while they were fighting?* It was Banni's habit to come up with questions of this sort whenever the LTTE came to Malini's school for recruits, and usually Malini answered by saying, 'Yes…no…maybe…I don't know,' but today she simply stayed silent. A sense of a disaster waiting to unfold had settled on her heart. She had never before seen such undisguised grief on her father's face. He had always hidden his true feelings. She wanted to talk to her father and ask him if he knew something that she didn't know about the direction the war was taking.

What she really wanted was some reassurance, but she doubted that her father would have anything of that sort to offer her.

Malini's house was a three-bedroom bungalow built by the British ages ago as a residence for the school's principal. Malini's mother, who took her Tamil responsibilities more seriously than her husband and daughters, had set up no fewer than three shrines honouring twenty household gods – twenty out of the thousands worshipped by Hindus – and had draped half of the walls in the house with tapestries from Madras showing many of the heroes of Hindu sacred literature. All the same, the house kept its English character, with its fireplace and mantelpiece and its parlour off the kitchen.

Malini's room – and this was where she was now waiting for her father's return from the school, waiting and reading, restlessly, for the third time, an English novel by Emily Bronte, *Wuthering Heights* – was far less gaudy than Banni's, which was decorated with posters of pop stars and pictures of the characters from Tamil soap operas. Malini's walls were covered with posters of famous writers purchased online from a shop in Bombay – Tamil writers, English writers, American writers, Sinhalese writers. Also a big poster of the periodic table of elements, and another with the title *The Eleven Most Beautiful Maths Equations*. None of the pop stars that adorned Banni's room. Malini also kept a small, personal shrine to Shiva in her room, with little plates of rice placed at the God's feet as offerings. When she refreshed the plates, she never asked any favours for herself, only for those suffering in the war. Her first task when she arrived home – before she picked up *Wuthering Heights* – was to ask Shiva to watch over the boys who been taken from the school that morning.

She heard her father enter the house. She stopped reading and waited for him to drink the fruit juice her mother would have ready for him, then gave him further time to kiss Banni, who would be in front of the television, then sit at his desk in his study and enjoy a little rest. Ten minutes after his arrival home, Malini went to the study door, knocked, and asked permission to enter.

She first kissed her appa on the cheek, then, with a comb from her pocket, made his long, greying locks neat. It was an affectionate ritual between them, this combing of her father's hair. She would also straighten his tie before school in the morning, and make sure that the tip of a white handkerchief protruded from his coat pocket, in the English fashion. Neat hair, a straight tie, and a handkerchief in the pocket were things that Malini's amma barely noticed. She reserved her adjustments to her husband's appearance for those sacred days of the Hindu calendar when he dressed in traditional Tamil costume – pattu vetty, a long silk cloth worn like a sarong and tied at the waist.

Malini said, 'Appa, is it true that LTTE will win the war this year?'

'No,' he said, 'it is not true. Not in 2008.'

'Next year?'

'No, Daughter, not this year, not next year. But if you ask me whether LTTE will lose the war this year, my answer will be different.'

'Will the Tigers lose the war this year?'

'Yes, Daughter. The government troops have entered the stronghold of the Tigers in the north. The Sri Lankan Army are fighting total war now. They do not care how many civilians they kill. They are more fanatical than the Tigers. But as the Tigers lose more of their stronghold in the north, they will become like madmen. These are our brothers and sisters in the faith and I pity them with all my heart. They are doomed.'

He took Malini's hand. 'They will lose. And it will be horrible. It will be horrible.'

Chapter 2

The soldiers came at dawn.

Malini was awakened by the noise in the town. She knew by the gunfire that soldiers had come, but she didn't know if they were Sinhalese or Tamil. Six months had passed since her father had predicted that the LTTE forces would be overwhelmed by the government troops, and she knew that the Tamil Tigers now stood on the brink of defeat. What they might do in their desperation was something her father worried about every day.

Malini wondered if this might be the Tigers now. As she hurried to comfort her sister, there was a loud knocking at the front door.

Her father, without great haste, attended to the knocking.

Banni, sitting up in her bed, asked her sister what was happening.

'We don't know yet. Stay calm.'

'I am calm. Why do you say "stay calm" when you can see that I am already?'

'Okay, good.'

The voices at the front door carried clearly to Malini and Banni.

First, her father's. 'What is your business?'

And then, a stranger's voice. 'How many in this household?'

'Why do you ask?'

'How many? *Answer!*'

The stranger spoke Tamil, but not the local dialect.

'Four,' said her father.

'All of you outside – now!'

'Why?'

'Why? Because if you ask one more question, I will kill you. Get moving!'

Malini and Banni waited in silence until their father appeared at the doorway of the room. Behind him followed their mother, still dressing herself rapidly in her blue sari.

'Kanavar,' their mother addressed her husband, 'who has come to our house?'

'Tigers. We have to leave. Malini, Banni, dress yourselves as quickly as you can.'

Banni started putting on the garments she'd worn the previous day – blue jeans, a pink blouse and Nike trainers.

Malini hurried back to her bedroom, took her second-best sari from the wardrobe, pulled off the long T-shirt she wore as a nightie and began expertly to turn the silk cloth about her body. Why take the trouble when she had jeans of her own? Because she had a strong feeling that she was about to die, and was indulging a sudden urge to farewell life as a Tamil.

Outside, the LTTE soldiers drove people into the town square with blows and curses. Those who faltered and fell were kicked where they lay until they staggered to their feet again. The soldiers seemed to be in a state of hysteria, as if they couldn't afford to lose a second moving people from their homes into the centre of the town.

Malini thought the soldiers looked so young, some no older than ten or eleven, not yet old enough to grow a beard. The lieutenant was much older than his soldiers. He wore reflecting sunglasses so that his eyes were concealed, and a bushy moustache in imitation of the famous Tiger commander Velupillai Prabhakaran. He was standing on the bonnet of a bullet-riddled Nissan four-wheel drive, shouting at the top of his voice, 'Assemble in the square. Assemble in the square immediately!'

A man in a white linen suit and small round-rimmed spectacles being urged forward by a soldier called to the lieutenant. 'I am a doctor. What is the meaning of this? You can see that the children are frightened. Explain yourself!'

The lieutenant said, 'You'll find out soon enough.'

The crowd in the square grew bigger and bigger, until there were perhaps as many as half of the town's population of 2300. Some had brought possessions with them, small things such as framed photographs and cooking pots. One woman had an electric toaster, for some reason; another, a teapot. Many of the children carried soft toys – SpongeBob, Garfield, Barney the Dinosaur. Faces everywhere in the crowd were streaming with tears. Mothers attempted to comfort their children; fathers shouted at the soldiers who were shouting at them. But the lieutenant in his sunglasses shouted louder than anyone. 'Stand closer to each other. I want everyone in the square. Everyone! If you make trouble, I promise I will shoot you!'

Malini's family was squeezed in along the edge of the square, against the brick wall of the Great Wonder Cinema.

Malini's father was held in high regard in Satham, and someone in the crowd appealed to him for an explanation. 'Honoured sir, what is the business of these barbarians, may I ask?'

By the time the Tiger commander was ready to address the crowd, the hubbub had grown so loud that he fired his rifle into the air. He called at the top of his voice, 'Do I have to shoot someone to make you listen? Do I have to shoot all of you?'

The crowd grew quiet. Malini's father, with one arm around his wife's shoulders and the other around his young daughters, drew them all closer.

'You are going for a holiday,' shouted the lieutenant, 'to Ankapur.'

An immediate rumble of dissent came from the crowd. Malini's father said, not loudly, as if to himself,

'This is bad.' Ankapur was a small village on the coast, some thirty kilometres away. There was nothing there but a couple of fishing boats.

'You are going to Ankapur,' the lieutenant shouted once more. 'All of you!'

'What is this nonsense?' the doctor called back. 'Ankapur? It is the heaven of mosquitoes – we will be eaten alive!'

Malini whispered to her father. 'What does he mean?'

'They want us as human shields, Malini. They will crowd everyone in on the coast, hoping that the government troops won't attack them for fear of killing civilians.'

'Will the government troops attack?'

'Yes, they will.'

By now, the soldiers had encircled the crowd: some standing on the roof of the Great Wonder Cinema, some on the roof of the courthouse, some on the back of the trucks that had brought them to Satham. A young soldier, a boy of no more than thirteen, stood on a low stone wall close to Malini and her family. The expression on the boy's face was frightening – fierce and heedless, as if he might at any minute go berserk and fire his weapon into the crowd. Malini nudged her father and nodded towards the soldier.

'What's wrong with him?' she whispered.

Malini's father glanced at the soldier. 'Drugs,' he said. 'The government soldiers use them, too. Don't make eye contact with him.'

The soldier made Malini think of a boy from her school, Thiaku, who had been conscripted by the Tigers at the age of twelve. He came back to the town after two years away. He had lost a foot on the battlefield and was no longer expected to serve. Some of the boys of the town considered him a hero and would sit with him and beg for tales of the war. He never said a single word.

Malini had seen him one morning on her way back from the market, sitting on a bench outside the old courthouse built by the British a century ago. His crutch rested beside him and he was staring straight ahead. Malini sat quietly beside him. After five minutes or more of silence, she noticed that tears were forming in his eyes. She'd waited longer, then asked, 'You have seen terrible things?'

Thiaku had glanced at Malini, then lifted his hands and held them out, staring fixedly at them. 'Do you see?' he'd said. Then he'd slowly hoisted himself up and taken hold of his crutch. He'd struggled away towards the part of the township beyond the courthouse, where he lived with his parents.

The next day, Thiaku had vanished from the town.

Malini, in the days that followed, thought of those three words: *Do you see?* Her enthusiasm for the war had faded away and never came back.

Malini's father climbed up onto the low stone wall surrounding the cinema to report what was happening on the far side of the square. The soldiers appeared to be driving people, in groups of around fifty, onto the road to the coast. It was mayhem. Children were shrieking, adults shouting out to their family and friends as they attempted to stay together. The soldiers fired their weapons into the air again and again.

Beside Malini, an old woman sat down on the ground and dropped her head onto her chest. 'Kill me here,' she called out. 'What do you want? I walk all day and then die? I will die here!'

Malini's father, fearful of what the boy soldier might do, helped the old woman to her feet. 'Say nothing, mother,' he whispered to her. 'Say nothing. Endure.'

Malini and her family, at the back of the square, were among the last to be forced onto the coast road by the soldiers. Malini heard her father whisper to his wife, 'We are in a trap. We can't even try to escape. If they shoot a few of us, it won't matter to them.'

The sun was now high in the east, and father, mother and daughters shuffled onto the coast road and began a journey that Malini hoped wouldn't end with the death of all of them.

Chapter 3

More and more people from the outlying villages around Satham were forced to join the thousands already on the road. Some were praying, some crying. Malini acknowledged with a nod or a bleak smile her many schoolfriends in the crowd. Some looked unkempt after rushing out of bed; others seemed completely demoralised. Keeping close to her father and her mother, she glanced at the two soldiers nearest to her.

'Keep moving,' they shouted over and over, as if they were singing the words of a harsh, unending song. 'Keep moving! Don't stop! Keep moving!'

I have never been more frightened of this war than I am today, Malini thought, remembering something her father had once told her: *When a war is ending, that's the most dangerous time.*

Malini kept a tight hold on her sister's hand. Banni was whimpering softly, past pretending that she was untroubled with being awoken at dawn and forced to leave her home, her DVDs and her video games behind. Malini's mother made no effort to hide her tears. Her father circled his wife's shoulders with his arm.

'Our home, Chandran,' Malini's mother whispered. 'Will we ever return?'

Malini's father replied, 'I cannot say.'

For the sake of her mother, Malini said, 'We will return,' but she had grave doubts.

When Malini was much younger, she had been known in her family as 'All-will-be-well' because of her optimism. Her father used to tease her. 'Malini, a meteor is heading for the earth! But all will be well, don't you think?'

The older Malini wasn't such an optimist. She had followed the war in the newspapers and on television for some years now, and she knew that some of the worst things in the world had happened in her Sri Lanka, episodes of terrible barbarity of which both sides were guilty. She had lost the innocence that had once made her say, smiling brightly, 'All will be well!'

The roar of an aeroplane overhead brought the crowd on the road to a halt. Someone called out, 'Kadavul kapatra vendum, God save us!'

The most feared aircraft were the fighter-bombers that appeared far away in the sky but then only a few seconds later were above you, so fast and so loud, like the roar of a typhoon.

This was a smaller aircraft. As Malini watched, sheets of paper spread over the sky, like an enormous flock of white birds descending as one to the earth below. Malini knew what these papers were. They'd been raining down twice a week for the past month. Each sheet contained a message to the people beneath, written in Tamil: *The Government of Sri Lanka guarantees the safety of all unarmed Tamil people. Do not enter the no-fire zones!* And there would also be a picture of an automatic rifle with a cross through it.

The Tamil Tigers were thrown into a frenzy by the arrival of the sheets. They shouted, 'Do not touch them. Leave them on the ground. Do not touch them!'

One of the soldiers close by even fired his rifle at the fluttering sheets as they flapped in the air. Banni shrieked and buried her face in her mother's sari. Malini dropped to her knees and whispered, 'It's nothing, Banni – just noise. Don't be scared.' But the truth was that Malini was very scared herself. The wild looks on the faces of the soldiers made her realise that things could go from bad to worse in the space of a minute. A frightened young man with a gun, Malini knew, could do a great deal of harm.

Some of the soldiers were attempting to snatch up the sheets as they fell, in order to destroy them: they tore them apart, or dropped them in piles and set fire to them. Their task was hopeless. There were too many messages hanging from the branches of the rhododendrons and the taller sapu trees on either side of the road.

'Keep moving,' the soldiers shouted over and over. 'What are you doing? Keep moving!'

As the crowd on the road began to shuffle forward again, raising red dust that settled back down on them,

Malini's father whispered to her, 'Do you see what is happening, Daughter? It is as I thought. They will use us as shields. I'm sure of it.'

Malini could tell from her father's expression that he had more to say.

'Look up ahead,' he said, 'where the trees come close to the road. Do you see the place I'm talking about?'

'Yes, I see.'

'When we reach that point, I want you to take your sister and steal into the trees. Be quick. Once you are in the forest, hide yourself. Do you understand, Daughter?'

'But what about you and Amma?' said Malini. A sick feeling was spreading through her body. She glanced at her mother. Red lines ran from her eyes down to her chin, dust covering tracks of tears.

Her mother said, in a faltering voice, 'Malini, do as your father says.'

'But what will we do in the forest?' said Malini.

'You must use your wits, Daughter. You will hear from me,' Malini's father said as he slipped into her hand a small bundle wrapped in the big white handkerchief that he always kept in his pocket. 'It's my phone and the charger. Don't look now. Later – when you are safe.'

Malini's feeling of sickness rapidly changed to panic. She couldn't leave her mother and father. Tears stung her eyes. 'Father, I can't.'

'Daughter, for the sake of your sister.'

Malini's mother bent quickly and kissed her on

the forehead, then Banni. Her father placed one hand on the head of each daughter and whispered a prayer that called on Vishnu and many ancient heroes of the Tamil people to protect his daughters. The aeroplane overhead had circled back and was dropping more messages. They'd reached the trees, and with the soldiers distracted, Malini's father said, 'Go now. Go now, Daughter!'

Malini tightened her grip on Banni's hand. 'Come with me. Say nothing, Banni. Nothing!'

Chapter 4

Where the cinnamon trees reached out over the road, Malini bent low with her sister's hand in hers and scurried into the forest's understorey of ferns and marga shrubs. From a tall malaboda tree hung a dense length of lichen, known as old-man's beard. This provided a perfect screen and Malini bustled Banni behind it and sat with her sister clutched to her chest.

Banni asked, 'Malini, what are we doing?'

'Shh, Banni. This is what Appa wants us to do.'

'Are we escaping?'

'Yes, Banni, we're escaping.'

'But I want Appa and Amma to escape, too.'

'They will, but not right now. Be still.'

The tramping of the people on the road and the shouting of the soldiers went on for another hour. Malini softly counted each minute as it passed, encouraging Banni to join in. 'One fat elephant, two fat elephants, three…' What Malini really wished for was the freedom to cry her heart out. Her father had told her, 'You must use your wits,' but Malini didn't feel clever; no, she felt like Banni must – desperate to be in arms of her father and mother.

Malini decided they should remain behind the lichen screen for a further hour, just in case. Banni had to be shushed every so often. 'I'm thirsty, Malini. I'm hungry. When can we go home?'

To distract her sister, Malini whispered, 'Let's see what Appa has given us.' She pulled out the bundle from inside her sari and unwrapped it. It was, as her father had promised, their spare mobile phone and also the charger.

Malini put the phone to her cheek as if it were her father's hand.

Banni grabbed at it. She probably wanted to play Buzz, her favourite game that was installed on the phone.

'No,' Malini snapped. 'Do you want to use up all the battery? Are you that selfish?'

Banni looked as if she'd been slapped – something that had never happened to her in her life. Her lips began to tremble and she threw back her head and wailed.

'No, Banni. No noise.' Malini covered her sister's mouth with her hand and kept it in place until she was sure that Banni would be quiet, but the instant she took her hand away, Banni let out an almighty shriek.

'Banni, shush! People will hear you.'

'I'll make the soldiers take you to jail!'

'Listen to me, Banni. This phone is very precious to us. And very important. You know what happens when the battery is flat? We can't talk to Appa when he calls us.'

Banni pointed at the charger. 'Fill it up again!'

'Yes, but where? We need electricity.'

'At our house!'

'Banni, we can't go back to our house. The soldiers will see us, and they'll be angry. We have to wait in the forest until Appa calls us and tells us what to do. And, if you are a good girl, there'll be sweets.'

'When?'

'When what?'

'When will there be sweets?'

Malini had no chance to answer. Gunfire sounded from the east, where the coast lay. A minute later, trucks rumbled down the dirt road. Malini glimpsed soldiers in the back of the trucks with their rifles pointing skywards, government soldiers in their green and khaki jungle-camouflage uniforms with gold badges on their berets. Malini counted twelve trucks, and two other vehicles with machine guns mounted on the backs. She could guess what was about to happen, and it filled her with dread. The SLA soldiers would attack the Tamil soldiers from land and sea, maybe from the air, too. The civilians who were meant to act as human shields, her mother and father included, would be caught in the crossfire.

Malini stared at the phone in her hand, willing it to ring. As she waited, the sound of gunfire increased. Banni was gazing at her solemnly, expecting comfort or guidance of some sort. It struck Malini like a blow that she was all that stood between her sister and the danger of the world. She did not want such responsibility.

'Why are there guns?' Banni whispered. 'What's happening, Malini?'

Malini didn't respond.

'When will there be sweets?'

Malini sighed and shook her head. 'I don't know.'

Tomorrow Malini would have started her birthday week. She would have bathed in the part of the river set aside for women and girls, washing her hair in the current to bring out the shine. Once her hair had dried, her mother would have plaited flowers into the long locks and made her a belt of blooms for her waist. She would have performed a dance in the back garden of her house with her girlfriends, and everyone would have called to her, 'Malini, Malini, your dancing does you honour!' Then the guests would have called on Malini's father to read a verse from the great Tamil poets of bygone days, and he would have replied, 'But what verse can do justice to this daughter of mine who excels in mathematics and geography?' Then he would have read the verse, with tears in his eyes.

Malini was wrenched back to the here-and-now by Banni, who whispered, 'Do you hear something?'

Two loud planes roared eastwards across the sky – fighter-bombers.

Banni put her hands over her ears. 'I don't like them!' she squealed.

'Nobody likes them,' said Malini.

She quickly murmured the Prayer of Destination for those starting a long journey, and hurried her sister into the shadows of the forest.

Chapter 5

Malini knew that anywhere close to where the Tamil soldiers and the civilians were trapped was dangerous. Government soldiers were ready to shoot quickly. If they accidentally shot civilians, there would be no reprimand. Heading inland – far away from this battle – was the only option she could see. She must travel west until she reached the highway that ran from Trincomalee all the way to Kandy and Colombo. Then she could get her bearings again, and keep going west to Ulla Alakana, the village of her appappa – her father's father – in North Central Province.

Appappa was her only relative who lived far from the fighting. She had once visited him with her parents, and with her knowledge of Sri Lanka's geography – one of her favourite subjects at school – she thought she might be able to find the village again. The journey might take weeks and every step would carry her further from her mother and father. But what else could she do? She wanted to be as close as possible to her father and mother, not leaving them further and further behind. But Appa would expect her to find what safety she could. She felt she must head west, even if she hated the idea.

'Do you know what we're going to do, Banni?'

'Find Amma and Appa?'

'Yes, but that will be later. For the next few days, we're going on an adventure. A big adventure.'

'Like in my Snow White book?'

'No, not like Snow White. Like in the stories Appa tells us of our Tamil heroes.'

'Will we have swords?'

'No swords. Just us. We'll sleep under the stars and see amazing things.'

Banni looked at Malini doubtfully. She was only eight years old, but she wasn't easily fooled.

'I want to stay here,' she said, perhaps for no other reason than to test her sister's temper.

'Well, we can't,' said Malini, abruptly abandoning diplomacy. 'And that's that.'

Malini took her sister's hand and gazed ahead into the trees and vines. The forest was full of tracks left by generations of people harvesting the spices planted beneath the canopy of the taller trees – cinnamon, pepper and nutmeg – but Malini doubted that these tracks would last. The further she went from the coastal region, the more difficult the journey would become. She was trusting to good fortune to find her way to the big highway and beyond.

It was now mid-afternoon. Malini took her bearings from the sun's position in the western sky and started into the forest with her sister complaining that her shoes were hurting her. Malini said, 'If sore feet are the only hardship we face, we'll be lucky.' Then she remembered that this was supposed to be an adventure. She stopped and crouched down with her hands on her sister's shoulders. 'Sweetheart, listen to me. When we finish this adventure, Appa and Amma are going to be so proud of you. So let's be brave. Okay?'

'*Sweetheart?*' said Banni, scornfully. 'You never call me sweetheart!'

'Well, I am now!'

Malini moved through the shadows of the trees wherever possible. For the first hour, Banni kept grumbling about her sore feet, her empty stomach, the insects that settled on her face, and the twigs that made a mess of her hair.

'When I tell Amma what you made me do, she will punish you,' Banni said.

'Will she?' said Malini. 'We'll see.' Banni's carping was a burden that Malini had to add to the grief she felt over the separation from her father and mother, but she had already promised herself that she would stay patient with her. Now she told herself, *It isn't her fault that she's so spoilt.*

Banni had always been pampered and treated like a princess. Malini's mother had lost two children between Malini and Banni – one, a boy, was stillborn, and the other, a girl, suffered from a problem with her heart and died at the age of two. When Banni was born so full of health, Malini's mother treated her as a great gift. Just as Malini's father sometimes teased Malini, so he would tease her mother about her way of doting on Banni. 'Oh, the Princess Banni is calling! Hurry, Wife – see what can be done to please her!' To Malini, he said, 'She is the beauty of the family. You are the brains. Brains last longer than beauty.'

As the afternoon wore on, Banni stopped complaining and instead began to cry softly. Malini found a place sheltered by trees and undergrowth where they could rest but still stay hidden. She sang softly to Banni, first a folk song that her father loved about a monkey who thinks the crescent moon is a huge banana, then a pop song by Miley Cyrus.

Malini thought, *Songs are well and good, but what will we eat?*

By this time, Banni had fallen asleep. Malini looked fondly at her younger sister. Most of the worst things that the war had brought to Satham had been hidden from Banni. She didn't know that innocent people had been murdered by soldiers. She didn't know that villages had been burned to the ground. Before today, she had never seen the anger on the faces of young men with guns in their hands. It was no wonder she thought of all that had just happened as a big nuisance.

Spotted doves and magpie robins were cooing and chattering in the branches above. One of the magpie robins hopped down, one twig at a time, and stared at Malini with curiosity. She loved the feathered creatures of her island, one of the great havens in the world for birds of so many species. In happier times, she had sat in the back garden of her family's home with her father to watch the birds on the boughs of the cucumber trees, the puwak palms and pudding-pipe trees. Her father would say, 'Do you know what the birds are thinking, Malini, my love? They are thinking, *Those poor creatures without wings! What a woeful life they lead!*'

From out of nowhere, a kingfisher flashed by, its blue plumage brilliant in the slanting rays of the sun. Malini called, 'Oh!' Then she said, 'So beautiful!' Without intending to, she had woken Banni, who immediately began to sob once more.

'Banni, I saw a kingfisher! The most beautiful bird in the world.'

'I don't care!'

'If there is a kingfisher, there must be a stream nearby. Come, we'll find the stream and drink some water.'

'I want Pepsi.'

'Yes, but not today. Today, we drink water.'

Banni reluctantly followed her sister through the trees. The two girls were off the path now. Every few steps, Malini stopped and listened, trying to pick up the sound of running water. And whenever she stopped to listen in this way, she also caught the distant sound of heavy weapons – she tried not to think about what that meant.

The stream was swift and clean. The water jumped over the rocks as if in delight at its freedom. Malini helped Banni down to the bank, then showed her how to cup the water in her two hands and drink it down.

Banni had great difficulty and spilt the water down her blouse. 'I want a cup,' she cried.

'No cups today, Banni. Here, watch me again.'

As Malini bent over the stream, she glimpsed something on the other bank that made her stop and stare. At first she couldn't find what she thought she'd seen in the dense foliage that came right down to the water's edge, but then, with a start, she saw it again, and there was an added surprise: what she'd imagined must be a statue half buried in the leaves and ferns became a living man.

He was sitting completely still in a cross-legged position, his long grey beard reaching down to his waist. He looked very old, his face deeply lined. Malini might have grabbed Banni and run for her life, except for the expression on the man's face. He wore a huge smile and in the light that reflected off the water, his eyes twinkled.

Banni was still grizzling about not having a cup. Without taking her eyes off the man, Malini reached behind herself and held Banni by the shoulder.

'Banni,' she said, 'look and see who is here before us at the stream.'

Banni looked. 'Ayya. Eppadi irukkinka, how are you?'

Malini had thought her sister would be alarmed at the sight, but then she realised that this was the holy man, the sadhu, who came now and again to Banni's school to bless the children. Malini had glimpsed him only once, more than a year ago, but she knew he was a man who enjoyed laughter, and that he was also considered a genius among magicians; he would thrill the schoolchildren by making rocks float in the air and flames appear on his fingertips. He could call birds down from the trees, wild birds that had never known captivity, and by some skill make it appear that they were reciting poems that told of the deeds of ancient heroes. When they knew he was coming, the children would bring small gifts of food. Their mother, a very frugal woman who watched her purse closely, would throw off all restraint when she prepared food gifts for the sadhu, providing Banni with the best cashews and the most succulent melon she could find in the market. She would roll up a broad banana leaf and tell Banni to flatten it before the sadhu and place the nuts on one side and the melon on the other.

The old man called across the stream. 'Banni, the moon girl. I see you there.'

He came quickly to his feet and walked through the rushing stream as if he were travelling on a paved road. Once on their side of the stream he placed the flat of his hand on Banni's head and tilted his own head to one side, as if listening.

'Oh, the thoughts in this moon girl's brain box!' he said. 'Strange and wonderful.'

Banni said, 'What am I thinking? Tell me what I'm thinking.'

'You are thinking of Pepsi. You are thinking of guava and coconut roti. You are thinking of television. Yes, all of these thoughts are in your head!'

Banni shrieked with delight. 'It's true! But you

must punish Malini. She makes me walk when my feet are sore.'

The old man laughed and wagged his finger at Banni. 'Punish this brave girl? No, no, moon girl, not in a million years of my life.'

Malini smiled. 'Thank you,' she said. 'But why do call my sister "moon girl"?'

'When the full moon shines,' said the old man, 'Shiva comes and leaves this child gifts in her heart.'

Malini put her hand over her mouth to hide her smile. 'Are you sure it is to our Banni that Shiva comes?' she said.

'Oh yes, indeed yes,' said the old man. 'One day she will surprise you.'

Banni said, 'Make a Pepsi come with your magic. Make coconut roti come.'

'To make Pepsi come to the forest is beyond my power, moon girl. But I can make vadai, fritters, and beetroot pachadi, salad, come to the forest.'

The old man bent down and picked up Banni as if she were as light as a kitten. 'Come,' he said. He stepped into the stream with Banni in his arms, and Malini followed. The bed of the stream was covered in loose stones that slipped under Malini's feet and so the old man held out a hand to her, holding Banni securely with just one arm. The water rushed against Malini's legs, but she felt no fear of being swept away while the sadhu held her hand.

Once across the swift water, the old man lowered Banni to the ground. He picked up a smooth stick, as white as bone, which he had left on the bank and that served him as a staff. He parted the ferns with the stick, revealing a path. He led Malini and Banni along the path until it crossed a second path, and there, where the two paths met, stood a shrine of stone and wood dedicated to the god Shiva. The god sat cross-legged, with eyes closed in meditation, arms extended. At the foot of the shrine small pottery dishes filled with food had been left by travellers as offerings to the god. Not all of the food looked fresh, but the rice cakes did, and the dishes of guava.

The old man pointed at the food and said, 'This will restore your strength.'

Malini was horrified. To take food that had been left as an offering would be a sacrilege. Everybody knew that. Malini hadn't realised just how strange the sadhu was.

'We are not permitted to steal food from a holy place,' she said.

The sadhu stood before the shrine and spoke. 'Shiva, our life, may these children partake of this splendid guava at your feet? Shiva, our life, may these children enjoy the rice cakes left at your feet?'

A deep voice came from somewhere above, higher than the treetops. 'With all my heart!'

Malini gasped and took a step back from the shrine. But Banni shrieked with laughter and clapped her hands. Malini looked at the sadhu, then at Shiva. The shock she felt was not to do with the god speaking from the sky. No, it was to do with the sadhu using his magic to make it appear that the god had spoken.

'Oh, Ayya,' she said, 'but this is disrespectful, surely!'

The sadhu knelt before Malini and put his hands on her shoulders.

'My girl,' he said, 'do you think the Lord Shiva would wish children to go hungry when there is food at his feet? Shiva, who loves you like Ganesha and Kartikeya and Ashoka Sundari, his own three children? He would not wish that. Now eat.'

Banni seized a rice cake and devoured it. Malini, whose table manners had always been impeccable, picked up the guava and ate it slowly. Despite what the sadhu had told her, she still felt uneasy.

The old man asked Malini what destination she had in mind.

'My grandfather's village of Ulla Alakana. It is many kilometres away.'

The old man said, 'It is the war that you're fleeing, child?'

'Yes, the war.'

'And your honoured father and mother?'

'They are trapped in the fighting.'

The old man shook his head and walked in a small circle, stamping his feet. 'This war is a curse for everyone,' he said. 'Even the victors will suffer.'

He pointed with his white stick to a path that led through the forest. 'Go this way,' he said. 'And on your journey, listen for footsteps. Shiva will follow you. But do not turn from your path. Do not look back.'

Now he placed the palm of one hand on Banni's head, and the other on Malini's. He spoke the words of a language Malini had never heard before. Then he produced from the folds of his garments an earthenware bottle with a wooden stopper. He removed the stopper and offered the bottle to Malini.

'Before you go,' said the old man, 'you must refresh yourself.'

Malini tilted the bottle and drank down the cool water. It tasted as if it had come from the purest stream of a tall mountain. The old man took the bottle and handed it to Banni.

'First, close your eyes,' the old man said to Banni, and she did as she was instructed. 'Now sip.'

Banni sipped once, twice, three times. She was smiling when she lowered the bottle. 'Pepsi!' she said.

Malini resumed their journey with an aching heart. The time she'd spent with the sadhu had reminded her of how good it felt for someone else to take responsibility, how good it felt to be cared for, and loved. Her cheeks were wet with tears. She said to herself, *I do not have the strength for this. I am only fourteen years old.* But a minute later, she'd had a rethink. *Only fourteen, so what? Just get on with it.*

Banni was cheerful after their refreshments of rice cakes and guava. She chattered happily. 'When we reach Appappa's house, he will say, *Oh, precious child, my heart soars when I see you!* He always says that when he comes to our house. He will say, *In all the world, is there a child as beautiful as Banni?* It's true that I am very beautiful, isn't it, Malini? Malini?'

'Hmm? Oh yes, Banni. Of course.'

Malini came to a sudden stop. She held up her hand to caution Banni.

'Shh, Banni. Something is wrong. Be quiet for a minute.'

A strong smell of burning filled the air. Dense forest concealed the way ahead, but Malini could just make out the charred trunks of mesua trees.

'Banni,' she said, 'listen to me. Wait here. Sit on the ground and make yourself small. Put your arms around your knees. Don't come out of hiding until you see me.'

The carefree look had fled from Banni's face. 'Don't leave me here!' she said.

'Banni, do as I say. *Now.* I'll come back in a minute.'

Malini crept between the trees, pausing every few seconds to glance around. How used to stealth she had become in just a single day! It was as if she had trained for years to move invisibly in and out of shadows. Malini wondered whether the war did this to people – made them wary about everything. At first she hadn't even trusted the sadhu!

She could glimpse before her an open area where small flames flickered. The smell in the air was very strong – not just the smell of burning, but of fresh earth mixed with the tang of sulphur. Overhead, the broad leaves of the tall trees had been stripped away.

She ventured further, then stopped on the lip of a crater torn in the earth by what must have been a bomb. The raw earth still smouldered in places. Whole trees had been ripped apart and lay in fragments around the crater. But why had the bomb been dropped here, in the middle of the forest? Malini's father had told her that sometimes when the LTTE air wing of light planes had very little fuel, they'd be forced to drop their bombs before they reached their target to lighten their load. Malini thought of the destruction such a bomb would have caused if it had landed on a house, or on people – too dreadful!

The western sky was streaked with the crimson of sunset. Evening was settling in. A forlorn feeling came over Malini when she returned to Banni, alone with her sister in the forest without a morsel of food, without water, without shelter. They had been walking for hours.

Banni began to whine. 'Malini, take me to the toilet. I must go.'

'Behind those ferns,' said Malini. 'We are in the forest, Banni.'

Banni looked horrified. 'Take me to a proper toilet!'

'Banni, things have changed. We must make do in this new world.'

Malini realised that shelter was the pressing need. Walking further tonight seemed futile. She gathered her strength, scrambled down into the bomb crater and scooped out a shallow ditch. It would provide a little warmth, maybe, if they cuddled up. Banni had emerged from behind the ferns and was watching with a baffled expression.

'Come down here, Banni.'

'I don't want to.'

'Do as you're told!'

Banni clambered down into the crater reluctantly.

'Tonight,' said Malini, 'we sleep here in these ditches. Animals will keep away. They'll be suspicious of the smell of scorched earth.'

Banni settled herself into the ditch with evident disgust. Malini unwrapped her sari and used it to cover her sister. Left with no defence against the chill of night but her short-sleeved blouse and her underwear, Malini wriggled herself closer to Banni's body, only to be shrugged off.

'Don't suffocate me!' Banni complained.

Malini struggled for the comfort that would bring sleep to her tired and aching body. But before she allowed herself to relax, if relaxation was possible at all, she checked the mobile phone to see if she had missed a call from her father. There was no signal at all.

Banni whimpered, 'When will we eat?'

Malini answered, not quite honestly, 'Kalaiyil, in the morning.'

Sleep came at last.

Chapter 6

Malini awoke at dawn. The clouds in the east towered into the sky. Birds were calling in the forest – wood pigeons and bulbuls. The thing she was most aware of was the cold. She prepared herself for the first of the day's complaints from her little sister – probably to do with being hungry and dirty.

But when she turned over, she saw that the rest of the ditch was empty. Malini seized hold of the sari, left draped over the edge of the ditch, as if, impossibly, Banni was hidden beneath it. She leapt from the crater and shrieked her sister's name. Birds rose from the trees in alarm. Again and again she shouted, rushing first one way and then another. In her panic she even added a threat to her cries. 'Banni, if you are playing games with me, there will be a smack!'

Where would Banni go? Why would she leave the crater? Was it possible she'd been abducted? No, that was nonsense. This was Banni just being Banni, Malini hoped, finding every way she could to make her sister's life even more difficult.

Malini shouted until her throat was raw, then, in a lull between cries, she heard a girl's voice, singing. Malini stood stock-still, trying to pick up the direction. Then she recognised the song – it was the theme song from *Sesame Street*, a favourite of Banni's when she was younger.

Relief flooded through Malini like warm honey.

Banni strolled out of the forest towards Malini with a garland of wildflowers in her hand.

Malini kept her temper, just barely. 'Banni, you mustn't wander away like that. You made me sick with worry. Why didn't you answer me when I called you?'

Banni smiled innocently and pushed a strand of hair back from her forehead. She held the wildflowers out to her sister. 'Mannikkanum,' she said, apologising. 'For you.'

'Thank you,' said Malini. 'That's a lovely thing. But did you hear what I said about—'

'I wanted to do something nice for you,' said Banni.

'Something nice for me?'

'Yes.'

Malini felt guilty. This was the thing about Banni: she could be a nuisance all day, then suddenly do something so sweet and charming that you felt bad for scolding her.

Malini wrapped herself in her sari and tied on her sandals. She had eaten so little, yet she wasn't hungry. Her anxiety about her parents had taken away her appetite. She said to Banni, 'If I can find you some food, I will. But will you be brave until then?'

Banni said, 'I am always brave.'

The two sisters set off along the forest path, Malini holding in one hand her little garland of wildflowers.

Malini knew that if she started their journey from the heart of the island and chose to go north, south, east or west, they would come to a village within an hour. Her island home, carpeted with small villages, had been settled for thousands of years, and for most of those years, people had grown the food they needed in fields just beyond the fringe of their villages. Many villages were self-sufficient. Within each small community, someone would weave, someone else would have learned carpentry, and yet another villager would know about medicinal herbs. A bone-setter would go from village to village, tending to fractured limbs; a travelling dentist would pull teeth. Villagers usually lived their whole lives in the place where they were born.

Each Tamil village was under the authority of a council of elders, and that council itself was headed by a village chief. Malini knew that if they entered a village on their journey to Ulla Alakana, the chief would take her and Banni under his protection. He would not allow the two girls to wander back into the wilderness in search of their grandfather. Nobody knew what was going to happen now that the war was coming to an end: families scattered all over the place might never find each other again.

But the problem of food was becoming urgent. How could they walk all that distance without nourishment? Malini didn't know the answer, but she decided never to surrender herself and Banni to a village chief. She told herself, *Keep to the plan. Then we have a chance.*

Banni's good mood didn't last. She went silent for a time, then stopped and sat on the ground. Malini had to coax her to her feet.

Overhead, rainclouds were gathering from the east. The sun became a pale yellow disc lost in the mist.

Banni said, in a strangely grown-up way, 'It's too much. I'm only a child.'

Malini said nothing for a minute or more. 'Banni, in a war there are no children. There are only those who die and those who live.'

'I don't care if I die.'

Malini put down her garland and threw her arms around her sister. 'Never say that. Never, never. At this very minute, Amma is thinking of you. She's saying, *Dear Lord Shiva, keep my baby safe.*'

Banni shook her head. 'I don't care.'

Malini stroked her sister's hair and murmured soothing words, thinking, *Where will I find food? Where?* And as she thought this, her gaze was fixed on something green on a tree a way off in the forest. She didn't know what she was looking at for a time, and even when she saw the mango clearly she still thought, *I cannot be seeing what I think I'm seeing.* Mangoes often grew wild, but to find one just at this moment was astonishing.

Malini seized Banni's hand and hurried into the forest, right to the base of the mango tree. 'Do you see, Banni?'

Banni had another talent, apart from complaining: she could climb like a monkey. The trunk of the mango tree, though fairly smooth, had branches sticking out all the way up. Banni scampered up. She braced herself in a cleft, twisted the mangoes from their stems and dropped them, one by one, down to Malini. The mangoes were not fully ripe, but they would do. Then she paused. 'Sister?' she called.

'The last one, Banni – throw down the last one!'

'Look!'

Malini turned to see a child, perhaps as young as four, standing a few metres away. Malini gasped, but she was more curious than frightened.

'Who are you?' she asked.

The child said nothing. Barefoot and dressed in shreds of clothing, he or she – it was impossible to tell – stared first at Malini, then at the mangoes out of eyes that glittered with the fever of hunger.

'I won't hurt you, poor thing. Tell me your name.'

The child – Malini now thought him to be a boy – took two wary steps forward, then stopped. He was in a wretched state. Wood lice crawled in his bushy hair and his bare legs were almost as thin as Malini's wrists.

'Where do you live?' asked Malini.

Not a word came from the child.

Malini knelt down and opened her arms. 'Come,' she said.

The boy took one more cautious step forward, then, without warning, darted past Malini, snatched up a mango and sped off into the shadows of the forest.

'Chase him,' Banni cried from her perch in the tree. 'Thief! Thief! Shiva will strike you dead!'

'Banni, stop it. Get the last one and come down.'

Banni dropped the last mango then scampered down the trunk. 'We must find that demon and punish him,' she said. 'This is our tree!'

'Banni, it is not our tree. We found it by good fortune. That boy was starving. Perhaps he didn't have the strength to climb like you, and he was waiting for the fruit to fall.'

Banni, indifferent to her sister's sermon, was tearing open one of the mangoes with her fingers. She scooped out the yellow flesh and stuffed it into her mouth. Streams of juice ran down her chin.

Malini opened her own mango. She worked the thick skin into a hump with her thumb, then peeled it back, using a small stick to loosen the flesh. Banni had eaten two whole mangoes before Malini had finished half of one, and was about to start on her third.

'No,' said Malini. 'We save two for later. Have some forethought! With you, it is all about the present moment.'

Carrying the two mangoes and her bouquet of wildflowers, Malini led her sister along a path that descended through satinwoods and thorn bushes. It was Malini's guess that the path had been beaten by animals coming down from the forest to a source of water – a spring or a rivulet.

She halted suddenly when she came across the skin of a mango. This must have been the track the boy had taken.

Banni said, 'Hah! When I find him, I will punch him hard with my fist!'

'You will do no such thing, Banni.'

Malini slowed her pace, following fragments of mango flesh in the grass. The boy must have eaten the fruit without stopping. But where had he come from, and where was he going? Did he come from a village? If he had, Malini knew she would have to be cautious. She didn't want to stumble into a village, and then not be permitted to leave.

Fat drops of rain had begun to fall. Within five minutes, Malini knew, the sky would turn white and the rain would tumble down like water pouring from a cauldron. And although the rain was warm, if you got soaked it brought sickness and fever. The only shelter that Malini could see was the cover of the satinwoods, but the satinwood leaves were not broad, and even sitting against the trunk they would be drenched if the rain lasted more than ten minutes.

Better than nothing, Malini thought. She hurried Banni off the track through the tall grass and into the forest. Together they sat huddled beneath the bushiest of the satinwoods while the rain gathered force. A roll of thunder tore the sky open, and a minute later the intensity of the downpour doubled.

Malini tried to shelter her sister with her own body.

Banni shrieked, 'I don't like it! Make it stop, Malini!'

The roar of the rain on the foliage of the trees was deafening. Malini had to shout into her sister's ear. 'Be strong. A few more minutes and it will stop.'

And then she saw the strangest thing: through the blur of the tumbling rain, three children appeared, each holding the hand of another, their outlines barely visible. The children skirted the big satinwood that sheltered Malini and Banni, all in rags, all as thin as sticks. The child who was leading — a girl, taller than the other two, perhaps twelve years old – stopped still and stared at the two sisters huddled against the trunk of the satinwood. Malini made a beckoning gesture with her hand, inviting the children to take shelter, small as the space was. The girl seemed to consider, staring straight at Malini, who called, 'Come. You must! Come!'

Still the girl held off, perhaps struggling with suspicion, but then, as if a silent agreement had been reached, the three children crowded under the satinwood, pressing themselves against the trunk.

Banni cried out, 'Pooh! They stink!'

'Your manners, child,' Malini admonished. In the custom of her Tamil people, she gestured with clasped hands in sincere welcome. The haunted eyes of the children remained fixed on Malini's face, as if kindness itself aroused both wonder and wariness.

When the rain ceased, it ceased completely.

Malini, Banni and the three children sat in silence, listening to the forest as it shed the remains of the downpour, a musical series of notes as droplets higher up fell onto leaves below.

Malini had recognised that the children were not Tamil but Sinhalese. The girl had spoken a few whispery words in Sinhala to the younger children, both boys. Malini's father had made sure that both Malini and Banni had learned Sinhala.

Malini said to the girl, 'We are fleeing the soldiers. I am Malini. This child with the bad manners is my sister, Banni. You follow Lord Buddha, isn't that true?'

The girl made no reply, but she had understood – Malini could see that.

Then, Malini said, 'How is it that you are here?'

The girl averted her eyes, but said nothing.

'Have you suffered?' said Malini. 'You have nothing to fear from me.'

She reached for the girl's hand, and held it. The boy who had stolen the mango gave a yelp of fear, as if Malini were about to take the girl prisoner.

The girl told him, 'Calm yourself!'

The two mangoes that Malini had carried with her from the tree were being closely guarded by Banni, who was watching the newcomers with sharp suspicion.

The boys were staring at the fruit.

Malini reached for one of the mangoes.

'No! Let them find their own tree!' Banni said.

'Banni, we will share.'

With great reluctance, Banni handed one of the mangoes to Malini, and Malini gave it to the girl.

'Eat,' said Malini.

The girl sliced the mango open from top to bottom with her thumbnail, stripped it off its skin and allowed the boys to scoop the flesh into their mouths. The children ate noisily, moaning with pleasure. The girl did not eat, but watched silently. Malini thought, *She has the same task that has been given to me.*

Malini reached for the second mango.

Banni cried out, 'No!'

'Yes.'

Banni, with tears in her eyes, gave the last mango to her sister, who handed it to the girl.

The girl again sliced the mango open and tore back the skin. But this time she held the fruit out to Malini, who took a small portion, and to Banni, who shook her head in refusal.

'You won't eat, Banni?' said Malini.

'Her hands are dirty.'

The girl smiled. 'I am sorry for my hands.'

Banni had spoken in Tamil, and the girl made her reply in Tamil. Banni stared in surprise. The girl ate some of the fruit, then passed the mango to the boys.

After they had eaten, beneath the satinwood with the sky clearing above, the girl responded readily to

Malini's questions. Her name was Nanda, and she was not as guarded and suspicious as she had seemed at first. But, even in her more talkative state, Malini thought, there remained something slightly on edge about her. She rubbed her hands together and kept reaching up to her face to touch her cheek. And her eyes darted constantly, from the two boys to Malini, to Banni, and back to the boys.

Nanda told a harrowing tale. She had been moved from one orphanage in Colombo to another since birth – she had never known her mother and father. Two years ago, a charity with its headquarters in Australia had taken fifty children from orphanages in Colombo and made a rural home for them in the North Central Province. The idea was that the new orphanage would grow its own food, and the children would be taught how to raise crops and how to read and write in Sinhala and English. They would emerge from the orphanage ready to make a living other than begging.

But the war was never far away. At the orphanage, Nanda had been given some responsibility as she grew older. The children called her Mama.

'It was so hard,' she told Malini. 'All of those children without love, all wanting me to be the mother in their lives, and so many times I had to find a place by myself to weep.'

Two months ago, men came to the orphanage with a notice saying that it must be shut down. The men did not wear uniforms. They had two trucks to take the children away. The orphanage officials protested, and one known as Master, a kind man, was immediately shot dead. Panic broke out. Nanda was thrown into the back of one of the trucks, but during an argument among the soldiers, she grabbed the two boys and sprinted into the forest.

'I saw that the men wanted to do something bad,' said Nanda. 'I saw it in their eyes. This was an orphanage, but they had come to use their guns.'

Nanda hid in the forest with the boys. She heard gunfire, she heard explosions and she saw the smoke, black smoke, climbing high into the sky.

'I stayed in the forest for three days. We went back when I was sure the men had gone. I was full of fear. I was shaking. I did not want to see what I knew I would see. But it was worse than I had imagined.'

The orphanage had been burned to the ground. Only some stone walls still stood. There were bodies to bury – all of the orphanage officials; five children.

'We made shelters in the ruins,' said Nanda. 'I knew the men would not come back. We have lived for weeks here. Nobody comes. We eat roots, grass; sometimes we find wild fruit. Gayan came to that tree a few minutes after you. You must excuse him for taking your mango.'

Malini told her own story, while Banni sulked.

Nanda said to Malini, 'God willing, your trials will come to an end now.'

Malini said, 'Nanda, you will die here if you stay. I'm sure of that. There are no Sinhalese villages in this area. Poor child, you must come with my bad-mannered sister and me to Ulla Alakana.'

This was too much for Banni. 'Never in my lifetime!' she said, mimicking a phrase their mother used.

The boys seemed to listen closely as they chewed on the skin of the mangoes. Malini doubted that they understood Tamil, but they may have been picking up a few words. She could see how easily their thin bodies could succumb to an illness. And except for their thin bodies, the boys were no longer children – robbed of their innocence by having witnessed things so frightening that they were shocked out of childhood.

Nanda looked away from Malini. Her hand went up to her cheek and rubbed at it, as if she were trying to remove a mark. Nanda had seen such terrible things, and yet she had such a beautiful face! Whenever she averted her gaze, she looked as modest and shy as a village girl who had never been beyond the front door of her house.

She spoke to the boys briefly in their native Sinhala. One of the boys remained silent, looking down at the ground. The second shrugged.

'We will come,' said Nanda. 'Malini, Banni, will you hear the names of these children?'

'Please,' said Malini.

As Nanda gave the name of each boy, she reached out and lifted the chin of the child she was introducing, forcing him to look Malini, then Banni, in the eye.

'This one is Amal. He is five years old. Do you see the scar on his neck? He was in a fight in Anaradhapura. An older boy cut him. Amal has a good voice for singing – it's true.'

Nanda switched to Sinhala to ask Amal if he loved singing. 'Aetta-da, is it true? Boru-da, false?'

'Naeh,' said Amal, 'no.'

Nanda had embarrassed him. When she urged him again, he slapped her on her knee, hard, and buried his face in his thin arms.

'When he knows you better, he will sing to you about the Lord Buddha and the old woman on the mountain. It is a children's song. And this one is Gayan. He has been in too many orphanages to count. He is eight years old.'

'Eight!' Banni blurted out. 'I thought he was four.'

Malini put a finger to her sister's lips. 'Shush.'

Banni's surprise was understandable. Gayan, although elder, was the smaller of the two boys. Malini had noticed that he walked with a limp. Speaking Tamil, which Malini realised the boys couldn't follow, Nanda explained in a rapid whisper that Gayan had seen his whole family murdered when he was three – some shot, some hanged. In his headlong escape from the massacre in his village, he had fallen and broken his leg. It had never been set, and was now permanently crooked.

Malini attempted to stroke Gayan's rough tussock of hair, but he struck her hand away and burrowed into Nanda. Banni snorted in disgust.

'Then we are together,' said Malini, turning to more immediate problems than Gayan's rejection. 'What we will eat, I do not know. But what we find, we will share. Is that agreed?'

'It is agreed,' said Nanda.

Banni said again, 'Never in my lifetime!'

Nanda showed Malini and Banni the ruins of the orphanage. A signboard that had survived the fire now formed part of the wall of a shelter. The words read: *Children of Lord Buddha, in Whose Wisdom we trust forever.* The rain had roused the stink of burning, even weeks after the fire. An iron wood-oven sat unevenly on its four stout legs in the charred debris of what must once have been the kitchen. Nanda showed Malini the steel frames of classroom desks, all the timber burned away. She said, 'It was the best orphanage in our whole land. There were three classrooms and a special room that we used as a temple. Even the smallest children learned to revere Lord Buddha. Our teachers were kind to us, especially Master. They did not run away when the men came.'

Eleven graves lay outside the perimeter of the ruined orphanage. Nanda said, 'We buried them. We had no shrouds, so we covered them in leaves then put earth on top.'

Malini said, 'The men who came – were they Tamil or Sinhalese?'

Nanda said, 'I don't know. Maybe they were bandits. They spoke both languages. Whoever is their god, they did not bring Him with them.'

Nanda and the boys gathered what few possessions remained to them: two spoons, a short-bladed knife, a soft toy kangaroo that had somehow escaped the flames, and a set of coloured pencils in a tin box.

'And this,' said Nanda. From beneath a stone wedged against the base of a satinwood, she produced a wad of cloth. When she unwound the cloth, she revealed a number of thousand-rupee notes.

'But Nanda,' said Malini, astonished at what Nanda was displaying, 'why did you not buy food in a village? You have thousands of rupees here.'

'If such a person as I entered a village, the money would be seized from me and I would be locked away.'

'The men who came here did not find the money?'

'Master hid it. I knew where to look.'

Malini thought for a minute. 'If I could find a way, would you permit me to buy food with this money, Nanda?'

'With all my heart.'

They set out on the road that led west. Not that there was a road, or even much of a track. Malini and Nanda walked ahead, the children following. Banni insisted that the ragged orphans keep their distance from her. Whenever they encroached on her space, she turned and gestured for them to observe the rules. 'Do not come close to me. Do you hear?' she admonished in Sinhala.

Amal and Gayan smiled at these admonishments. But they played the game.

Malini's thoughts were all to do with a strategy for

buying food. Ten thousand rupees would feed them for a month. But unless she was clever, she would get nothing; the money would be taken from her, and she would be confined by the village chief.

'Nanda, did peddlers ever come to your orphanage?'

'Many times,' said Nanda. 'They had cloth for sale and a hundred things – spices, rice, ornaments, even toys. They will never come again.'

'No, Nanda, they won't. But the track that leads to the orphanage must join up with a road that the peddlers use. Let's find that road.'

Chapter 7

When Malini found the road it was not much better than the track that led to it, but that was what she'd expected. The peddlers she had in mind plied their trade in small villages and travelled in bullock carts. They were the last of the old-fashioned peddlers. The more modern peddlers got about in four-wheel drives, or trucks, and only visited the larger villages. The old-fashioned bullock-cart peddlers used to come to Malini's town when she was a small girl. She remembered the excitement of those days, the peddler, and sometimes his family, standing on the cart as they displayed lengths of cloth, calling out the prices in song-form:

'Ladies, ladies, come to me,
Ladies, ladies, come and see,
A few rupees, a few rupees,
Silk and cotton, Tamil ladies,
Silk and cotton, buy from me!'

But would such a peddler come this way today, or even tomorrow?

Malini left Nanda and the children hidden in the forest while she waited near the roadside. Banni, of course, would not sit with the other children. She said to Malini, 'Tell them not to come close to me. Tell them not to speak to me. They are beggars.'

Malini sighed. 'We are all beggars.'

The traffic on the road was sparse. Pools of water lay shining in the dips and depressions. In the tree under which Malini was sheltering from the sun, a flock of bulbuls squabbled over seed pods. Whenever a motorcycle drove by, the bulbuls rose into the air, only to return to their squabbling when the vehicle had passed. The men on the motorcycles were not soldiers, just teenage boys going from one village to another. Still, Malini hid each time she heard a motorcycle. In Sri Lanka, a Tamil girl would never go wandering off by herself, never stand alone on a remote roadside. She would be thought badly brought up, or mad.

No peddlers came down the road on that first afternoon, nor the following day. While Malini watched at the roadside, Nanda made a shelter that kept the children dry when it rained. She found fresh water, a few wood apples and some fruit like a plum, but they had been pecked at by birds and were beginning to rot.

After dark, the boys huddled together. Nanda would not permit herself to close her eyes until Amal and Gayan were asleep. Banni slept beside Malini, and then only after Malini had told her a story about a brave, strong girl whose name was also Banni, but who possessed amazing powers. 'Famous Banni was so strong she could pull up trees by the roots and throw them at her enemies. Her strength came from a special drink that tasted like Pepsi. And how fast Famous Banni could run! Like the wind on the sea! And Famous Banni had a bow and arrow more wonderful than anything in the world. She could fire an arrow from one side of Sri Lanka to the other. All the birds of the air obeyed Famous Banni. She said, *Bring me mangoes! Bring me coconuts!* The birds would whoosh away and come back with one hundred coconuts and two hundred mangoes.'

Banni said, 'A bird cannot carry a coconut or a mango.'

'These were big birds. Serpent eagles. Now, the thing about Famous Banni that made everyone love her was that she would not eat a single piece of mango or a single piece of coconut until all her friends had eaten first.'

'What friends?' said Banni.

'She had many friends. Some Sinhalese, some Tamil, some Muslim, some Christian. Even some Jewish friends, like Mr Fonseka from our town. They all had to eat before Banni would take a single mouthful.'

Banni said, 'I know what you're doing.'

'Do you?'

'It won't work,' said Banni, and she curled up and fell asleep.

On the afternoon of the third day, when Malini had almost given up hope, a peddler appeared on the road. She saw the bullock wagon from a long way off and she heard the song of the peddler.

'Ho! It's the snail-man who carries his house on his back!
Ho! It's the snail-man who carries a shop on his back!
Ho! So many wares – who can count every one?
Ho! So many wares – who will buy every one?'

Malini stood in the middle of the road with her hand held high. She said, 'Ora nimidam, one moment!'

And the peddler, without missing a beat, immediately changed his song.

'Ho! Who says to the snail-man stop?
The snail-man and his shop!
Ho! A girl of the woods says snail-man stop!
The snail-man and his shop!
A strange day for the snail-man,
With his shop and his house on his back!
A strange day for me, my friends, with my shop and my house on my back!'

The peddler's wagon was brightly painted with images of many gods and goddesses, but foremost was Shiva on the back of a tiger with a bow and arrow. Ganesha, the Elephant God, sat on his throne with his four arms raised, a hatchet in one hand, a lotus flower in another, in the third a dish of sweets, and in the fourth a radiant gem. Buddha was shown, too, with earlobes hanging down lower than his chin. Malini knew it was not unusual for peddlers to decorate their carts with both Buddhist and Hindu images – everyone a peddler met was a potential customer, after all, whatever their religion.

The bullock that drew the cart was decorated, too, with necklaces of marigolds draped around his neck.

The peddler brought his cart to a halt and smiled down at Malini. He was an old man, although not as old as the sadhu, and his mouth was full of gold teeth.

'Young lady,' he said, 'the snail-man welcomes you to the world. For indeed the world is my garden. I have travelled to every land on earth, yes, even to the land of mist and snow at the bottom of our round planet. Or did I dream it?'

Malini said, 'Sir, I ask if you have rice to sell, and other food? I have money.'

The peddler raised both hands to the sky. 'Do you hear that, Lord Shiva? Lord Buddha, do you hear? The young lady of the forest has money for rice. But do I have rice for money? That is what she wants to know. Ho! I have cloth for a sari, braids for the hair of a Tamil lady, bracelets of gold for a girl's slim wrist, pots and pans, sandals and shawls. But do I have rice for rupees, that is the question the forest girl asks me!'

'Do you, sir? Do you have rice?'

The peddler raised his head and sang.

'The forest girl stands in my way!
The forest girl – what does she say?

61

The forest girl asks for rice!
The forest girl asks my price!'

Then he said, 'A bushel or a peck, forest girl?'

'A peck.'

'Why not a bushel?' said the peddler. 'There are five of you.'

Malini gasped. How could the peddler possibly know of the children hidden out of sight?

'Fi-five?' stuttered Malini.

'Fi-five,' said the peddler, and he held up five fingers.

Malini glanced behind her. But the children were still concealed in the bushes. She saw nothing.

'Why do you say five, sir?' she said.

'Why? Because I have learned to count in my many years, forest girl. Your eyes and eight others.'

Malini looked back at the forest. Now, she could just make out the hint of a face among the foliage.

'Come out!' she called. 'All of you – come out!'

Leaves rustled, and first Nanda then the two boys and finally Banni stepped out of the forest, all looking embarrassed.

'Your eyes are sharp, sir,' said Malini.

'My eyes are sharp,' said the peddler, 'and my wits are sharper, forest girl. You are running from the war?'

'From the war, sir, yes. This one is my sister, Banni. This one is Nanda. This is Amal and Gayan. I am Malini, sir.'

'And you have jumped from the forest to buy rice from the snail-man?'

'We have, sir. We can pay.'

'A bushel or a peck, forest girl?'

'How many rupees for a peck, sir?'

The peddler hummed a tune and gazed up at the sky, as if he were calculating the price.

'Let us say, one hundred and fifty rupees.'

'Yes, we can pay one hundred and fifty rupees, sir. May I ask, do you have fruit for sale? Do you have—'

The peddler cut Malini off. 'If it is to be found in the round world, forest girl, the snail-man has it among his wares. How many rupees can you afford to part with?'

As soon as Malini was placed in the position of spending a limited sum of money, she all at once turned into her mother. In Malini's town, her mother was famed as a woman who knew how to strike a bargain. With a mixture of charm and stubbornness, she squeezed every morsel of value out of a rupee. Malini's father – who always paid what a shopkeeper asked without a qualm – used to laugh and say, 'My dear, why not ask the man to pay *you* to take his goods?' Malini had always felt embarrassed to be at her mother's side while she haggled, but she felt no embarrassment when she bargained with the snail-man.

Over the space of an hour, Malini purchased two pecks of rice, potatoes, a packet of salt, dried chilli, six goose eggs, bananas, navel oranges, red apples, mangoes, rhubarb, honey, brown onions, roasted pepper, ginger pods, cumin seeds, cabbage, red pumpkin, a peck of dried lentils, ghee, a large bottle of Pepsi, biscuits, a tin of milk powder, eggplants, two deep saucepans, matches, a packet of plastic spoons, a big block of soap, two towels, a plastic hairbrush, a jar of antiseptic powder, five plastic bowls, and two sturdy carry-all bags with red, white and blue stripes. But Malini also saw the necessity of clothing Amal and Gayan in something other than rags. As it happened, the peddler had pyjamas for small boys for sale, and Malini could see that they would serve as day-wear in the heat. They were anything but traditional – bright yellow and orange, and printed all over with images of Bart Simpson on a skateboard – but they would do nicely. They were cheap enough to start with (they came from Bangladesh, and were made of the most inexpensive cotton) but not quite cheap enough for Malini.

She said, 'Sir, do you say three hundred and thirty rupees for the two, or for one pair?'

The peddler said, 'Forest girl, a demon lives in you. For one pair, three hundred and thirty rupees. Or do you wish all of my children to go hungry for a year? I have sixteen children, forest girl. Maybe more, I lose count. If I come back home with an empty purse, they will weep at my feet!'

'Sir, my offer is five hundred rupees for two pairs. I can afford no more.'

'Ai, ai! Why do I hitch my old bullock to this cart and travel all over our land of Sri Lanka? Why do I not stay at home and starve to death in comfort, myself, my honoured wife, my eighteen children! Are you mad, forest girl? Six hundred and fifty rupees. This price will not change until the sun turns to ghee and fills a bowl on my table!'

'Five hundred and fifty, sir. You can see the state of these children. Is there a heart in your body? I hope so, sir.'

'Six hundred, that I may find a quiet place where I can cut my own throat. Not one rupee less.'

'Five hundred and seventy,' said Malini.

'Ai ai! Nee ennai yemathikitu, you're cheating me! Take them! Leave me to my misery.'

But the peddler's trial was not yet over, for Malini next turned her attention to some clothing for Nanda. Among the peddler's strange assortment of clothes were a range of T-shirts emblazoned with the names and faces of Western pop stars no longer in their first flush of fame. The peddler must have acquired them at a discount from China or Bangladesh. Nanda chose a Bon Jovi T-shirt that came down to her knees, and also a pair of khaki shorts with six sets of pockets. And for Banni, to give her a change from her blouse, Malini chose a green shirt with short sleeves. By the time the peddler had gone on his way, Malini had spent five and a half thousand of the ten thousand rupees. She knew the prices of everything after years of shopping with her mother, and she felt quite proud of the bargain she had struck. Her mother could have done no better.

Now the five of them gathered their purchases together and retreated deep into the forest to prepare a meal. They found a place by a stream, well away from any paths. Before Malini set to work building a fire, she handed everyone an apple and passed around the Pepsi. Banni had to set aside her distaste for drinking from the same bottle as Nanda and the boys, but that took about two seconds.

Malini suggested to Nanda that she might like to bathe the boys in the stream. 'And yourself, if you wish,' she added tactfully. 'I must bathe, too, and Banni.'

Banni was put to work gathering wood for the fire, and she accepted the task without complaint. She had just seen Malini exercising the authority of a mother, and she seemed impressed.

Malini would usually bathe her arms up to the elbows, wash her face and brush her hair before preparing a meal – such was the Tamil custom, at least in her mother's kitchen. Then she would ornament her forehead with a fresh red pottu – a small dot, perfectly round, that symbolised the spiritual third eye of her faith. But this evening, she settled for scrubbing her hands in the stream with sand and tying her long hair at the back of her head with a strip of supple acacia bark.

As Malini busied herself preparing the meal, she began to hum a song. She could just glimpse Amal shrieking with delight in the stream as Nanda lathered his hair with the block of soap; Gayan, far shyer than Amal, washed himself. Banni, meanwhile, was building a circle of stones for the fire. Malini paused, and smiled.

Happiness had come to life in her heart. Somehow, a family had been assembled here in this wild place, and there was food enough for all. The pain of separation from her mother and father was easier to bear just for the moment. She thought, *Whatever is to come, however bad, let me remember this time.*

While the rice was cooking in the saucepan, Malini peeled a brown onion, cut it fine, and fried it lightly in ghee with slices of red pumpkin, potato and dried chilli. When the rice was cooked, she added salt and pepper then buried small pieces of mango in the rice to soften the fruit. Next she made an omelette with two of the goose eggs and the milk powder, cut it up and mixed it with the rice and mango. She blended in the red pumpkin, onion and potato, and left it to build in flavour while she softened some stalks of rhubarb to mix with banana slices and honey. When Amal and Gayan had finished bathing in the stream, they sat cross-legged around the fire in their Bart Simpson pyjamas and watched Malini. Nanda, who had bathed herself in private, joined them a few minutes later. Malini gave Banni the task of serving a heaped bowl of the main course to Amal and Gayan, then to Nanda.

Banni said, 'What, am I a servant now?'

Malini answered, 'Have you forgotten who paid for this food?'

When Banni, now a little ashamed, had finished serving, Malini blessed Lord Shiva and invited Nanda to bless Lord Buddha. Then they ate.

And what a feast. One of the boys, Amal, began to

weep even as he was filling his mouth from his bowl.

Nanda asked him, 'But Amal, where do these tears come from?'

Amal said, 'It is too nice, Mama!'

Then the rhubarb, bananas and honey.

The boys crooned with pleasure.

Another sip of Pepsi.

And the welcome prospect of breakfast awaiting them all when they awoke in the morning.

Malini checked the phone to see if there was a signal before she closed her eyes. No signal, and next to no battery. The blessing it would have been to have said just a few words to her father! Or even to her grandfather, except that there was no mobile coverage in his village; no telephones at all. Malini thought, *I will be grateful for the blessings I have. Oh, but Appa, how I miss you! And you, too, Amma. Both of you.*

Chapter 8

Malini and Banni luxuriated in the silky flow of the river's current. The sand was fine enough to scour their skin and hair, mixed with the lather of the soap. Though raised in the Hindu faith, they did not always observe the strict rituals of bathing. In their house, their father had built a modern bathroom with a bathtub and a shower where Malini and Banni washed each morning. But every week, they bathed at least once in the river, according to customs that had endured for two thousand years.

One of those customs was to bathe upstream from any other bathers who were not Hindu. Nanda, a Buddhist, had also been taught to bathe upstream from non-Buddhists, according to the customs of her faith. So in the morning, down at the river, there had been a problem: strictly speaking the river could not be shared. The single block of soap and the towels could not be shared by either. Malini knew that using the soap, the towels and the stream itself would all be considered unacceptable, but remembered the words of her father, who said to her one morning when a family of Indian gypsies crossed the bathing stream, thus polluting it, according to the more pious Tamils of the town, 'So the gypsies are not human beings, then? Malini my dear, our faith is a doorway to the universe, not a prison.'

When the sisters had dried themselves and dressed, Banni sat on a rock while Malini brushed her hair and told her more of the story of Famous Banni, who happened to be the most beautiful person on earth.

'And more famous than all the famous people,' said Banni.

'Of course!'

Banni said, 'Sister, sing me my song.' She meant the song Malini had made for her years ago: a song celebrating the beauty and wonder of Banni.

Malini, with some reluctance, began. 'All the people come to see, the treasure of our family...' Malini's song petered out.

'Go on!'

'No, that's enough. That song was for when you were an infant. You are too old for it now.'

Banni was about to shout at her sister, but something in the stern look on Malini's face stopped her. She said nothing for a minute. Then, quietly, 'Okay. I was sick of that song anyway.' Then she added, almost beneath her breath, 'I'm sick of everything. I want Appa and Amma.'

'What?' said Malini.

'Nothing,' said Banni.

Malini imagined that they must make a strange spectacle, traipsing through the forest: a tall girl in a sari leading the way, a smaller girl in jeans behind her, another girl in a long Bon Jovi T-shirt and khaki shorts, then Gayan and Amal in Bart Simpson pyjamas. All were washed and refreshed, all had brushed their hair. Anyone who didn't know their story might almost have thought they were on their way to some special event – a birthday celebration, or a day at the market.

The western track that Malini had chosen from three that diverged in different directions was perhaps too well-worn for safety. But she stayed alert, ready to herd her refugees into the forest at the first sign of strangers. It was mid morning before her nerve was tested. Nanda called to Malini, 'Wait!'

Banni, whose hearing was the most acute of all of them, had stopped dead on the track with her head raised.

Nanda said, 'Banni, what is it?'

'She hears something,' said Malini in a whisper.

'Hears what?'

'Four people,' said Banni. 'Ahead of us. Four.'

'Four?' said Nanda. 'How can he she tell? I hear nothing.'

Malini whispered, 'It's her special thing. She's usually right.'

The forest on each side of the track was dense. Malini could get everyone concealed in a few seconds if necessary. She said, 'Keep going,' but had no sooner spoken than a group of Buddhist monks in orange robes came around a bend in the track. Nanda, Amal and Gayan immediately clasped their hands beneath their chins. The monks walked slowly, weaving their shaven heads to the left and right, up and down, in the manner of birds. It took Malini a few moments to realise that they were blind.

The monk in the lead, an older man, came to a halt, sensing people ahead of him.

Nanda called to him, 'Sohoyura, sadarayen piligannawa, Brother, you are welcome.'

And the monk replied, 'Oba dhanagana lakema sathutak, pleased to meet you. Oba kohendha, Namgi? Where are you from, Sister?'

'Dhura,' said Nanda, 'far away.'

The monk explained that they were pilgrims, on their way to the temple at Somawathie, further south. 'We will turn off this road and find our way to the shrine,' he said.

Banni, fascinated by the sense of direction of a blind man, asked him how he would know when to turn. All of the monks giggled, as if Banni had said something hilarious.

'Everyone knows where Somawathie is!' said the monk.

The monks continued on their way. As they passed, first Malini, then Nanda and Banni and Gayan murmured words of parting, good wishes. But as the monks passed Amal, without the least warning, he began to sing. He stood with a straight back, his chin tilted high, and from his throat came a sound like a songbird of the forest. He sang Mahayana sutras, sacred verses that honour the teachings of the Buddha. The beauty of his voice, issuing from his skinny frame clad in Bart Simpson pyjamas, was startling. One of the monks turned his head, as if to acknowledge the beauty of the singing. When the monks were out of sight Amal stopped singing as suddenly as he'd started.

Banni, in her amazement, said to her sister, 'Did you hear that? He should be on television! He should go on *Sri Lankan Idol*!'

'Amal was raised by monks until he was four,' said Nanda. 'They taught him to sing.'

'Why did he not stay with the monks?' said Malini.

'The soldiers came,' said Nanda. 'They hanged the monks.'

Malini and Nanda each carried a candy-striped bag holding their food, utensils, and odds and ends. It was a struggle; the bags were heavy. This was the first time since the separation from her parents that Malini was free of worry about where the next meal was coming from. And yet, relieved though she was, Malini couldn't stop thinking of her parents. It had become her habit over the past four days to check the signal and the battery status on the phone tucked into her sari every hour or so. The signal fluctuated from medium to weak to non-existent, and when she'd last checked the battery an hour earlier, the screen was blank. She would have to use the recharger, which meant that she would first have to find a town with electricity or at least some place with a diesel generator. A big, big risk.

Wrapped in her thoughts, Malini was only dimly aware that the path she had taken with Banni and Nanda and the boys led steadily uphill with a valley below. She knew she was heading west, and that was all that mattered for the time – west to the big highway, across the highway and deeper into North Central Province towards the town of Galenbindunuwewa, then north to her grandfather's village of Ulla Alakana. It was only when Banni tugged at her arm and said, 'Look!' that she properly returned to the here and now.

Banni was pointing towards an almost sheer wall of rock on the far side of the valley. Down the rock face ran a waterfall that plunged into the river below. And the rock face ran for a long, long way upstream.

Nanda said, 'No bridge here. And the rocks are too big.'

This river must be Mahaweli Ganga, Malini thought. She had known that it lay ahead and was hoping to find a bridge. They would have to walk upstream to find a safe place to cross.

They followed the valley until the land sloped down to the river, and by noon found themselves on the bank. A break in the rock face on the far side meant that this was the place at which they would have to cross; a better place might never appear. But the river here was wide and fast-flowing. The boys and Banni would never stand up against the force of the current.

Malini said, 'Rest while I think.'

Nanda took care of the meal – oranges and Pepsi. Malini walked down to the lapping water to study a clutter of logs and branches that been had been trapped by an outcrop of rock. She picked up a piece of wood and threw it out into the stream. The current took the floating wood a little way downstream, but also across the stream towards the far shore.

What if a raft could be built, Malini thought, *and the children held tight to it and the current took them to the far shore.* Was it possible?

Malini called the boys and Nanda to her. 'Now you have to work,' she said, and she sent them up into the fringe of the forest to cut vines, as many as they could, and bring them back to her.

It was her idea to bind the logs and branches together with the vines; then the children could hold fast to the makeshift raft and let the current draw it to the opposite bank. The danger was that the raft would continue on down the river towards the sheer rock face, or that the children would lose their grip and be swept away.

Malini said to herself, *I should not take this risk.* But she was the only one worrying. The boys and Nanda, even Banni, all threw themselves into the project as if it were a fabulous adventure. The branches were hauled from the stream, laid out on the bank, lashed together with vines. Gayan, usually quiet and withdrawn, shrieked with glee as the raft took shape.

All the while, the sky grew darker. A storm was coming. It was on the tip of Malini's tongue to say, 'No, it's too dangerous. We will walk until we find a safer place.' That was what she should do. And yet she was reluctant to deprive the children of their fun. But if someone drowned, would they say, 'Don't worry, it was fun'?

The raft must have a name. Malini asked for suggestions. Amal suggested 'Warrior Boat That Kills Our Enemies', but Malini said no, the name must be a happy one that pleased all gods. Banni said, 'We will call it "Pepsi",' but that name, too, was turned down. Malini herself suggested a two-word name, made up by joining the Tamil word for 'peace' with the Sinhalese word for 'happiness', but this pleased no one. Finally Malini said they would give their raft an English name, for in history the English had enjoyed great success at sea. 'The Queen Elizabeth,' she suggested. Only Malini spoke English, however, and 'The Queen Elizabeth' was abandoned. With the storm coming closer, Malini accepted 'Warrior Boat That Kills Our Enemies', and the raft was pushed into the stream and held secure with two lengths of vine.

The two carry bags were made of a tough, waterproof fabric. Malini tucked her mobile phone and recharger into one of them, whispered a quick prayer, and fixed the two bags on the raft. Then she slipped into the river beside the raft – the water came up to her waist.

She called the boys to her, and helped them and then Banni onto the raft. It would be the task of Malini and Nanda to push the raft out into the current, hold it with both hands and attempt to steer it towards the far bank by kicking their feet. Malini knew she was a strong swimmer, but Nanda? Malini had not thought to ask her if she could swim. She did so, just as the raft was about to be pushed into the current.

'No, not in my life,' said Nanda.

'Then make sure that you hold tight to the raft,' said Malini. 'You are not scared?'

'Very scared,' said Nanda.

Rain was drumming on the river surface. Malini pushed with her feet and the current took hold of the raft and swung it out towards the middle of the stream.

Amal cried out with joy.

Banni said, 'Push harder!'

The raft moved slowly with its human cargo. Nanda kicked furiously with her feet. Malini called to her, 'Just hold on! Don't kick!'

Now Malini could feel the powerful tug of the current, and she knew instantly that she had made a mistake. The raft picked up speed and swung around, so that Malini and Nanda were now at the front.

Nanda was in danger of being pushed under by the bulk of the raft. 'Climb onto the raft, Nanda!' Malini cried.

Nanda hauled herself up and managed to struggle on board. The raft was now swinging wildly. The boys were still shrieking with delight, but Banni was holding on for her life.

The flow of the current brought the raft to the far shore, but at such a speed that it crashed against the bank and rebounded into the surge. When it swung into the bank again it caught against an outcrop of rock and Malini was able to find her footing and hold the raft steady against the pull of the current.

'Jump off!' she cried. 'Be quick.'

Nanda helped Amal onto the bank, but Gayan attempted to jump just as the raft tilted in the flow and he crashed into the water. Malini, holding the raft against the current, could only scream as the current caught him and bore him away.

Banni leapt from the raft into the river – what was she thinking, Banni who could not swim? – and by flailing away with her arms reached Gayan and held on to him. Malini, trusting the raft to Nanda's strength, swam to both children, seized them by the hair, and kicked her way to the bank.

Nanda and Amal strained to hold the raft against the rush of the river. But it became too much, and the raft tore itself from their grasp and swung back out into the current. Malini watched in horror, thinking of the phone. With Banni and Gayan safely on shore, she launched herself back into the river, overtook the raft with powerful strokes and held to it as it lurched and dipped. She was being carried down to the sheer rock face but she refused to let go of the raft. She could hear, dimly, the cries of Nanda, Banni and the boys, like the screeching of parrots. The raft smashed into the rock face, spun out into the middle of the river, then spun back and struck the wall again. This time, it wedged itself into a broad gap in the rock face. Malini, with barely a breath left in her, scrambled onto the raft, grabbed the carry bags and held them to her. The force of the current freed the raft from the cleft in the rock face and Malini, as sodden as a river rat, was again borne downstream. She held tight to the carry bags. 'Shiva, in your mercy save me – that is my prayer!'

Chapter 9

Banni stood wailing on the bank of the river, head thrown back, tears flowing down her cheeks and falling off her chin. Nanda and the boys tried to comfort her, without success. Whenever her wailing turned to words, all that came out of her mouth was, 'Sister! Sister!'

The rain had eased off and the heat of the sun raised steamy water vapour from every tree and bush. The last of the storm clouds sat on the peaks of the hills that reared almost sheer from the river's edge. Finches gathered to chatter in the ferns, as if attracted by Banni's howls.

But Nanda had her eye on a new mass of cloud sweeping in from the east. She urged everyone to shelter under a massive overhanging boulder, and the boys obeyed her, but not Banni, who was crying, 'Come back, Sister! Come back! All my bangles I give to you!' This was a serious sacrifice; Banni's bangles had been her pride and joy, but they'd been left at the house when the soldiers came.

The rain came down with such ferocity that Nanda was able to prevail on Banni to take shelter. But even under the roof of rock, she wept loudly and called on her sister to return. Nanda, who sat stroking Banni's hand, secretly doubted that Malini could have survived.

Banni seemed to read her mind. 'She will come back! I promise you.'

Nanda agreed. 'Of course!'

The rain fell so heavily that it formed a temporary waterfall, curtaining off the entrance to the shelter. Nanda feared a mudslide, or even an avalanche. She had seen it happen in the past: the rain loosened boulders, and the plunging stones knocked others in front of them. Even the boulder she and the children huddled under could be smashed by tumbling rocks. But what was to be done? Until the rain stopped, it was impossible to see more than an arm's length away. And she had to get the children dry as soon as she could. They were already shivering in their sodden clothes.

Dim though the light was beneath the boulder, Nanda could just make out a natural tunnel that appeared to lead upward in a gradual way. She climbed up to investigate.

The tunnel opened into a broader gallery, and Nanda had to judge whether it was safer for the children to remain where they were, or to risk moving them into the gallery. If a mudslide come down the mountain, it might entomb them, but if rocks came down with the mud, they might all be crushed under the boulder. She decided she would risk the gallery.

First, Nanda had to persuade Banni to retreat into the tunnel.

'And Malini? What will my sister think when she comes back and finds us gone? No! Here I stay!'

Nanda went out into the pounding rain. Above the bank of the river she made a big arrowhead shape with rocks, pointing towards the boulder. Then she took off her Bon Jovi T-shirt and attached it to a stick driven into the ground, so that it would act as a signal.

Nanda was putting on a show for the children's sake, trying to appear the very model of bravery and competence. But the truth was that she could barely hold herself together. Malini had come into her life like a blessing, and she adored her. She'd come to think of Malini as her protector. For the first time ever, Nanda had begun to believe that her journey through life might lead to some sort of haven. But now Malini was most likely dead. She was constructing a signal for a person who would never return. The full burden of the life she'd led before the comfort of Malini settled on her heart once more, and she ached in every muscle with grief.

With only her frayed singlet and her shorts to clothe her, she called Banni to look at what she'd done.

'Do you see?' she said to Banni. 'She will know where we are.'

'You will catch a bad, bad cold,' said Banni. Then she added, 'Nanda, I thank you.'

Nanda led the way on her hands and knees. Banni brought up at the rear, urging on the boys in front of her. As Nanda lifted her head to peer into the gallery, a thousand tiny lights came to life. She gasped with astonishment. The boys behind her baulked, not knowing what was happening ahead. Banni bumped into Gayan, and shrieked in Sinhala. 'Do I want your behind in my face?' she said. 'No, I do not!'

'I am sorry,' said Gayan. 'Truly, Banni, miss.'

'Shush!' said Nanda.

The lights were – well, what were they?

'Insects,' Nanda whispered. 'Like fireflies.'

Insects they were, luminous insects, but they looked like jewels. In their light, Nanda could just make out the dimensions of the gallery, and it was huge, enormous: ten houses could fit into the cavern. Pillars grew up from the floor and down from the roof, as if a temple had been constructed here by some strange race: built, then abandoned.

'Oh, children!' she called. 'This is magical!'

All alarm forgotten, the boys crawled over each other to reach the gallery.

'Aiee!' cried Amal.

And Gayan, his head raised in wonder, clapped his hands together lightly, as if in praise. He said, 'It is the home of Buddha. Oh, surely!'

Nanda wriggled her way from the tunnel into the gallery. She stood and gazed around. The other children joined her, Amal squeaking with the wonder of it all, Gayan gazing about gravely. The insects could not be seen, only their light, no matter how close they got to them.

Nanda took a cautious step, and another. Then she stopped. On the floor of the gallery lay the remains of a campfire: charred sticks, grey ash. And close by, a backpack and an open metal box full of cartridges. Nanda had seen cartridges like this before. The soldiers without uniforms who had come to the orphanage carried guns that fired rapidly and threw out shells of this sort. Nanda backed away, as if the cartridges were venomous snakes. 'Don't touch them!' she told the boys. 'Don't go near them!' An awful trembling came over her, and a sickness in the pit of her stomach.

The insect lights went out, not slowly but in an instant. Nanda reached out towards the boys and Banni and pulled them to her. They stood huddled close together in the darkness, scarcely breathing.

Amal whispered, 'Mama, what will we do?'

'Just stay still,' said Nanda. 'Let's sit.'

They sat still for an hour or more. Gayan, with his knees drawn up, buried his head in his arms and whispered over and over the brief phrase he always repeated in times of dread. 'I don't care...I don't care...I don't care...'

Amal had his own strategy for dealing with fear – a long, rambling story, also told in whispers, all to do with shooting his enemies and dropping bombs on their houses.

Finally Banni said, 'I am going back out to look for Sister.'

'Wait!' said Nanda.

A faint scraping sound was coming from somewhere within this underground world, right on the edge of hearing.

Banni whispered, 'What is it?'

'I don't know,' said Nanda.

'We must run!' said Banni.

'No. Don't speak.'

The boys hugged Nanda more tightly. Whatever was making the sound was moving towards them; with each passing minute, it grew a little louder. Was it a human sound? Nanda thought she could make out grunts of exertion. Gayan whispered, 'Mama, it frightens me!'

'Be still,' said Nanda. 'Be still and wait.'

A voice came out of the darkness, too: a boy's voice. What was the boy speaking about? Nanda heard the word 'elephant' distinctly, and 'birthday cake'. What in the world?

'...it was her birthday, you see...I have baked you a beautiful...lady elephant...Ha ha ha!'

Banni whispered, 'What is happening? Who is speaking?'

'I don't know,' said Nanda.

Chapter 10

The raft crashed into the rock face with such force that it split in half. On one half, Malini with the two carry bags stayed wedged against the rocks; the other half was flung out into the current and spun in a circle before disappearing around a bend.

The power of the rushing water was steadily nudging Malini's part of the raft away from the rocks. She gambled everything and heaved first one bag and then the other up onto a broad ledge above the reach of the water, then jumped into the river just as the current seized the raft and ripped it away from the cliff face. Malini's hope was that she could reach the tip of an overhanging branch before she was swept away. Shiva must have wished to honour her courage, for her grasp found a branch, and the branch held. Hand-over-hand, she hauled herself to the rock face and onto the ledge.

She lay there, gasping. When she regained her breath, she wept. She couldn't control it, howl after howl, and in the midst of her grief she called out, 'Appa! You can't ask me to keep going! You can't!'

If she was hoping for sympathy, she hoped in vain. The dense grey clouds above her opened and the rain came down in a torrent. She refused to move. She couldn't possibly get wetter than she was already. She thought, *Let the rain drown me. Let the stream take me. Let the world end for me. I will never find Appappa. I will never see Appa, I will never see Amma.*

Malini 'All-will-be-well' seemed further in the past than ever. But then her father's smile came back to her: the smile he had worn on the day she overcame malaria. Nine years old she was, shivering uncontrollably for days, shivering and burning at the same time and so weak that she could not raise her hand to hold a glass of water. A sadhu had come to her bedside to bless her in the life she was about to enter, the life beyond life. Her mother on her knees in the corner of the room had wailed her heart out, cry after cry. The sadhu had said, 'Everything here is finished for this child. She is awaited in another place.'

Malini had suddenly glimpsed her father hold up his hand as if commanding the sadhu to be silent. And she had heard his voice: 'The child is wanted here.' The next day, the shivering passed, the burning passed. She saw the smile on her father's face. And she heard his words, 'You are wanted here, my beloved.'

Malini roused herself. In her heart she sensed the grief that her sister must be feeling. It was almost painful, this rush of love for her Banni, the need to be with her, to hold her.

The rain stopped, all at once and completely, as it did in most of Sri Lanka. Malini climbed to her feet and tried to get her bearings. The cliff rose before her, far too steep to climb. She explored a little further along the ledge, arms spread wide and fingers clutching the cliff face as if they were claws.

She inched her way around a corner, and a second later was staring into the dark eyes of a boy in a Tamil Tiger uniform.

The instant they saw one another he cried out, 'Please! Sister, please!'

Malini's mouth opened in preparation for an almighty scream, but it stayed open without any sound coming from it. Rapidly she judged the danger she was in. The boy was seated on the ledge, which widened once around this corner. A gun lay across his lap, one of those guns that spat out bullet shells as it fired too fast to count – the soldiers who had driven her family from their town had carried guns like this. His right arm hung limply from the shoulder and the fabric that covered it was soaked in blood. His legs dangled over the ledge.

'Who is with you?' the boy asked. He was perhaps twelve years old, the same age as Thiaku, the boy soldier from Malini's town, when he had been conscripted.

Malini closed her mouth, but didn't open it again

to answer the question. She decided she was not frightened of the boy in the least. The gun, yes; this skinny boy, no.

The boy said, speaking the Tamil of the far north, 'Sister, help me or I will die here. You are of the faith. Do not let me die.'

Malini, hanging precariously from the ledge with her fingernails biting into the cliff face, was in no position to carry on a conversation. But she said, 'In my faith we don't kill people with guns like that.'

'I have killed no one,' said the boy. 'Not one person. I have never fired this weapon.'

'Throw it away,' said Malini. 'Throw it away and I might help you.'

'Throw it away?'

'Yes. Into the river.'

'Into the river?' The boy seemed close to tears. 'If my commander finds me without my weapon, he will shoot me.'

'Where is your commander?' said Malini.

The boy looked away, his expression dazed. 'He is dead.'

'Then he can't shoot you, can he?'

The boy didn't reply, but after a time he turned his gaze back to Malini. 'A soldier must not lose his weapon,' he said. 'It is shameful.'

'Then I cannot help you.'

The boy pushed the rifle from his lap with his good arm. It fell clattering down the rocks and into the river.

'There!' he said. 'Is that what you want?' There were tears in his eyes.

Malini said, 'What is wrong with your arm?'

'It is broken,' said the boy.

Malini left the other questions in her mind unspoken. It was plain that the boy was unable to move from where he sat. How he had managed to reach the place where he was now stranded, Malini could not imagine. But he would remain where he was until he died without her help. Or fall into the river and drown.

Shallow steps hacked into the rock led up from the ledge to an opening in the cliff face: six or seven steps that you would only be able to climb with two strong arms to steady yourself. Malini could see the boy's dilemma. He could not climb up the steps into what must be a cave, and he could not swim across the river with his broken arm.

Malini knew that she couldn't cross the river again with the two bags, but if she left the bags behind the children would starve.

She asked the soldier, 'Is there a cave at the top of those steps?'

'Yes,' he said. 'Very big. It goes all the way through the mountain and back to the river upstream.'

Ah, thought Malini, *Shiva has brought me to this cave!*

She said to the soldier, 'I will return to you.'

'No! I plead with you in the name of my mother!'

'Be calm, I will keep my word.'

Malini made her way back along the ledge to the

bags. She had the strength to pick up both at the one time, but the weight of two of them slung from her shoulders would make it impossible to get along the ledge. She would have to carry one at a time.

With caution, she succeeded, her shoulders aching. She dumped the first bag beside the soldier. 'If you touch the bag, I will leave you here for a hundred years. Do you understand me?'

The second bag was heavier. She was only too aware that a tiny stumble would plunge her into the river. And this was the bag with the phone inside. If she lost that, she would be happy to drown.

The boy was watching her get over the last part of the ledge with tears running down his cheeks. 'My thanks!' he said. 'All of my family honour you with their prayers.'

Malini unburdened herself of the bag and sat down on the ledge, completely exhausted. Once she had recovered her strength, she slung one of the bags over her shoulder and prepared to climb up the steps.

'I will carry these bags up to the cave,' she said to the boy. 'Then I will help you up the steps.'

The boy, still sobbing, told Malini that he didn't want to be a soldier, that he hated being a soldier, but that they had forced him.

Malini said, 'That's all very well. But if you can't be a soldier, at least try to be brave. I have enough children on my hands.'

'You have children?' said the boy.

'Perhaps. Now be quiet.'

91

The cliff face leading up to the cave was steep, if not sheer. With the weight of the bag hanging from her shoulders, Malini had to press herself to the rock, using the steps like a ladder, one foot below, hand reaching up, then the next foot and the next hand-hold. She wouldn't have believed it when she was scaling the cliff face, but once in the cave she had to admit it was worth the climb. The narrow opening to the cave betrayed how vast it was inside. The ceiling was as high above her as the top of a great satinwood. Stalactites grew down to the floor, while the stalagmites rose up and up. At this time in the afternoon the sun shone straight into the cave from the west. Malini stared about in wonder, murmuring to herself, *But this is a miracle, this is magnificent...*

She climbed back down almost to the ledge, one careful step at a time. In truth, she didn't know if she would be able to find the strength to help the boy up to the cave. She wondered what her conscience would tell her if she decided to leave him where he was. Because she wished she could leave him, she truly did.

She looked at the boy, who was gazing up at her with the eyes of a wounded puppy.

'This will be hard,' said Malini. 'I hope you have the strength. And I hope I do, too.'

She told the soldier to stand upright, put his foot to the first step and hold on with his good arm. 'I will lean down and take your hand,' said Malini, 'then you take the next step.'

The boy did as he was told. Malini, flat on her

stomach, leaned down as far as she could, almost half her body overhanging the lip of the cave. She grasped the soldier by the wrist. He took the second step, shielding his broken arm as best he could. At the next step he began to lose heart and wailed to the sky that he would surely die.

With even more wailing, the boy was at last able to struggle into the cave. The first thing he said when his breath returned was, 'Oh, miss, you are honoured by every god on the earth!'

'Lie on your back,' said Malini. She had taken the knife from the bag and was preparing to use it.

'I am Kandan,' said the boy. 'And your name, miss?'

'Call me "miss",' said Malini. 'That is enough for you, for now.'

She cut the sleeve of his camouflage shirt up to the shoulder. The blood on his upper arm had congealed, suggesting that the wound was not very deep. Nothing on the surface indicated a fracture, but Kandan screamed when Malini pressed her fingers against his upper arm. She cut the sleeve off completely, then tore it lengthways into three strips. She used Pepsi to wash the wound, dabbing at the dried blood with the hem of her sari. When she was able to see the wound clearly it became evident that it amounted to no more than a rough scratch. The bruising was the source of all the pain. She sprinkled some of the antiseptic powder she'd purchased from the peddler on the wound, bound it with one strip of fabric, then fashioned a sling with the other two strips. Kandan whimpered the whole time.

Even as Malini bound his arm, Kandan could not help glancing, between screams, at the open bag from which the Pepsi and the knife had been retrieved. With his wound bound and his arm in a sling, he again let his gaze slide towards the food on show.

'You must be hungry,' said Malini. 'How long since you've eaten anything?'

'Hungry? Oh no, miss! I mean, yes. But I cannot accept your food. Three days, miss. With no food. Three days.'

Malini had noticed what looked like a folded map protruding from one of the bulky pockets in Kandan's trousers. She said, 'I have an apple for you. And you have something I would like.'

'Anything, miss!'

'Your map.'

'I beg your pardon, miss?'

'You have a map. In your pocket.'

'Oh yes! Mannikkanum, sorry! I forgot about that. But it is six maps, miss, not one. Six maps that show the whole district. The captain gave them to each of us, but I could not understand them. They are not like proper maps, miss. They are military maps – a great mystery to me!'

Malini fished the wad of maps from Kandan's pocket, glanced at them and put them into one of the carry bags. Then she handed Kandan an apple. He devoured it, core and all, in thirty seconds. She gave him three of the hard biscuits. He crunched them down without drawing breath. She allowed him to drink a little of the Pepsi. Then she said, 'Tell me how you came to be here. Let every word be the truth.'

Kandan accepted one more biscuit and another sip of Pepsi. Then he told his story.

'We were conscripts, miss. Nine of us. Our commander was a captain. We came overland from the north to join the fighting on the coast. I did not want to be a soldier, but I had no choice. They wanted one from every family and my brothers were too young. My father said, *If you die, we are honoured. Be brave.*'

Malini interrupted him. 'How old are you, Kandan?'

'I am twelve years old. I should be in school.'

Malini shook her head.

'Miss, I did not want to die. I want to see my mother and my father again. I do not like fighting. We had no time for training. I can fire my gun, that is all. Many times the captain struck me on the head for crying, but I couldn't help it. I had to leave my rabbits behind. I had two English rabbits. I loved them, and now my mother will kill them and eat them. She thought they were foolish.'

'Rabbits?' said Malini.

'I know. My mother said every day, *This is nonsense.*'

Kandan began to weep. Malini wanted to laugh about the rabbits – she couldn't help herself – but she managed to keep quiet, and even patted Kandan on the cheek, as a mother would.

When Kandan had recovered, he resumed his story.

'We came on motorbikes: two on each bike, five bikes. We were seen by a helicopter with red markings. Do you know what that means?'

Malini said that she did not.

'Commandos. Oh, they are hard soldiers! They fired at us and our bikes ran off the track. We ran then, as fast as we could. I hid in the forest but I heard shooting. I ran again, deep into the forest. Then I found the top of this cave – up there.' Kandan pointed to the roof of the cave. 'I climbed down into the cave – such a wonder as I ever saw in my life! That was two weeks ago – I think, I'm not sure. I was too frightened to come out. I ate all my rations. Three days ago I had to find water to drink and I came to this place above the river. Someone had made steps in the cliff, maybe a long time in the past. I climbed down to the ledge but the rain began, very heavy. And before I could climb back to the cave, a stone came loose up on the cliff and fell on me and struck my arm. Aiee – the pain! And then I could not climb back to the cave. I thought surely I will die here, but then you came!'

Malini had seen young men from her town go off to fight in the war so full of confidence that they were telling stories of their bravery before they'd even seen an enemy soldier. Some of the boys, not all. The older ones, mostly. Young men could be turned into such dangerous creatures once a rifle was put into their hands! Those young men, they would do exactly what they were told, no matter how dreadful. But what of the conscripted boys who were like Kandan? No boy was ever ready for death – not for his own death, and not for the deaths he might inflict. Malini remembered Thiaku, whose soul had been destroyed by what he'd done, who'd looked at his hands and said, 'Do you see?'

But now it was time to find her way back to Banni and Nanda and the two boys. Malini packed the bags and told Kandan that he must lead the way to the opening of the cave upstream. 'You have one good arm,' she said. 'You will carry one bag, and I the other.'

Kandan was happy to oblige. As he led the way, one arm in a sling, the weighty carry bag slung over the shoulder of his good arm, he chattered without pausing, everything and anything that came into his head.

Malini, anxious about her sister and Nanda and the boys, told Kandan to be quiet for five minutes.

'Five minutes?' said Kandan.

'Yes.'

'Exactly five? Then I can talk again? Oh, miss, I enjoy talking to you so very, very much! When I was a soldier—'

'I said five minutes, Kandan!'

'Of course. Manniththu vidunggal, excuse me.'

Apart from talking an endless stream of nonsense, Kandan also had a talent for finding his way in the dark. Time and again he took Malini's hand and led her around an obstruction – sometimes a pillar, sometimes a dip in the track. Once he stopped and suggested to

Malini that she strike a match – he had noticed the matches in her bag.

'Strike two at once.'

Malini accepted the suggestion. The glow of the flame reached far enough for her to make out a long wall, decorated with paintings and designs. Some of the drawings clearly depicted animals, others human figures.

'What is this?' she whispered.

'Ancient people. Before our faith, and before the faith of the Sinhalese.'

'How do you know?'

'I read it in a book when I was in school.'

'You like books?'

'Very much.'

The first people of Sri Lanka, thought Malini. And she asked herself: *Did these first people fight each other? Did they make wars?* Probably. In a world so rich in beauty, people still made wars on each other; people made ugliness. It baffled her.

Now they came to a low passage that made it necessary for the two of them to crouch and drag the bags. Malini, by this time, had given up on keeping Kandan from chattering even though she contributed nothing more than an occasional, 'Really?' or, 'Is that so?'

'Miss, I have such a good joke for you!'

Kandan prattled on with a ludicrous joke about an elephant and a birthday cake. As tiresome as he could be, in some ways Malini was glad to know that a boy could have a rifle put in his hand, be instructed in murder, and yet turn his back on it as completely as Kandan had. She thought: *Let every boy in Sri Lanka keep rabbits, let every boy in Sri Lanka throw his rifle in the river.* And then: *I like him. He's an idiot, but I like him.*

Chapter 11

Nanda sat with her arms encircling Amal. Banni hugged Gayan. All of them were baffled by the voice. To attempt to scramble out of the cave now seemed futile. Whoever it was seemed to be making progress without light. Nanda thought, *If we stay huddled here, maybe we won't be seen.* With her foot she nudged the rifle cartridges as far from her as she could.

More sounds of struggle. But no laughter. The sounds stopped. Nanda could hear breathing from a short distance away.

'Sister?' shrieked Banni suddenly.

And, from out of the darkness, 'Banni?'

'Sister! We are here!'

A hand reached into the nook where Nanda and Banni and the boys waited in tense expectation. The fingers touched Nanda's face, felt its shape.

'It's me, Malini.'

Banni launched herself towards the sound of the voice.

'Sister! Oh, Sister! I have been praying for you with all my strength!'

Kandan lit a match, startling Nanda, Banni and the two boys. Gayan raised his hands as if to protect himself, and Amal shrieked, 'Demon!'

In the glow of the flame, Kandan's huge smile did in fact look rather demonic. His camouflage uniform also acted on Nanda and the boys, less so on Banni, as a menace.

'Oh, kalai vanakkam, good morning, children. I mean good evening. I am Kandan.'

'Who is that?' said Nanda, for Kandan had now crept closer.

'Don't be frightened of him,' said Malini, who was holding Banni close, 'He's harmless.'

The flame of the match died, but a moment later the luminous insects came to life again: the fireflies in their thousands. Malini, in her astonishment, murmured, 'All the Gods, what is this?'

In the faint light of the fireflies, Banni stroked her sister's face and sobbed as if she were suffering a fit of hiccups. Malini reached out for Nanda and the boys. Kandan, whose cheerful manner seemed to have convinced the children that he was indeed harmless, sat close by, not too close, saying over and over again in Sinhala and Tamil, 'Such a day!'

Stroking Banni's hair, Malini told the story of her escape from the raft, and of her discovery of Kandan. 'His arm is broken,' said Malini. 'Or injured. It's difficult to tell.'

Within the hour, Malini had moved her family, now including Kandan, down to the mouth of the cave and had managed to get a fire burning. Nanda's Bon Jovi T-shirt hung in the smoke on two sticks, gradually drying out.

Malini first served all the children and Kandan with hard biscuits, orange and apple halves, then with curried rice and eggplant. She was so exhausted after the ordeal of the day that her hands trembled with fatigue. Nanda said, 'Sleep, now, I beg you.'

Malini said no, she would wait until night, but in the end she lay just inside the mouth of the cave and slept a long, dreamless sleep until the stars came out. She lay listening to the sound of laughter. Kandan was telling jokes in Sinhala of the sort that only small children could possibly enjoy. 'Ho, ho, this one will please you! It is about a monkey and a parrot. One day, it seems, a monkey from the north met a parrot from the south...'

Malini fell asleep once more, and remained asleep until morning.

First, breakfast, then it was time for the children to be washed in the stream. Malini, scrubbing Amal with the bar of soap, holding him still and admonishing him when he squirmed, said aloud for everyone to hear, 'I am a mother before my time. And I will be an old woman before my time if this keeps up. Stay still, monkey!'

It was just a complaint, but not a trivial one: Malini felt herself ageing in a way she didn't enjoy. She feared that she would soon find herself carping and coaxing and laying down the law like an old village matron. How often in the past she'd listened with dread to her Aunt Talla, her father's sister, who would come to visit from Madras in India and spend the entire time shouting and smacking and giving lectures on the best way to bring up children. Malini's father would say, 'Oh, Malini, Banni, what joy is ours, we are to be visited by the Dragon of Madras!' And Malini had made this promise to herself: *I will never scold in this way of Aunt Talla's when I am a mother, if I have that good fortune. I will smile at my children, I will say, 'Enjoy life, every second of it!'* Yes, that had been her promise, but now there was no room in her head for anything but fret and worry. Yet another thing to hate about war! It robbed you of your sense of humour, robbed life of all colours other than grey and black, turned you into an Aunt Talla.

Malini lingered over packing for longer than she needed to, because the next thing she had to do – and this was awful – was to tell Kandan he could not come with them. If government soldiers found them, Kandan would be arrested, very likely executed, and Malini and the children would be regarded with great suspicion for being in his company. Malini called Kandan away from the games he was playing with the children and told him that he must try to find a Tamil village and take refuge there. Kandan listened without saying a word, but the expression on his face was one of utter devastation.

'Oh, this is the saddest news of my life!'

'Yes, Kandan, but you can see the danger.'

'Miss, I will hide if government soldiers come! I am good at hiding.'

'No, Kandan. I've made my decision.'

Malini had tried to keep their conversation secret, but the children were watching and could see that something was wrong. Banni had taken a great liking to Kandan, finding that he was easy to boss about, and now she hurried over to the riverbank where Kandan stood with his head drooping almost onto his chest.

'Sister, did you say that Kandan must stay behind? No! A thousand times no! He is our friend!'

'I have made my decision.'

'No! I forbid it!'

'You forbid it? You are a child. You will do as I say!'

Banni's eyes welled with tears. 'I will tell Appappa to strike you with a big stick when we reach the village. You are like a crabby old woman!'

Malini turned away from Banni to prevent herself losing her temper. What the child had said touched on the very fears that had vexed her earlier.

When Malini turned back to face Banni, she had regained control of herself.

'I am sorry we cannot take Kandan with us. It's too dangerous. We will leave him some food, but after that he must find a village where he can be safe.'

Banni walked away with her head bowed.

The parting with Kandan acted on Malini's nerves badly, probably because she felt so guilty for leaving him behind. She stood aside with a stiff, set expression on her face while Amal and Gayan and Banni hugged him and patted his hand. Kandan's tears fell from his cheeks in streams. Even Nanda, who had been standing beside Malini, rushed over at the last minute to put her arms around Kandan's skinny frame. When Kandan called to Malini, 'Miss Malini, always in my life I will remember you!' she shrugged and said, 'Yes, good, whatever you like.' Then she called out, more forcefully, 'Hurry up, all of you! Do you think this is a holiday?'

Malini led the way along the riverbank, with Nanda at the back and the three children in between. The landmark Malini was searching for was the great highway that stretched south-west from Trincomalee on the Bay of Bengal down to the capital, Colombo. Once it was recharged, the phone's signal would be stronger close to the highway. What she yearned for was just a brief message of encouragement: 'Keep going!' or something like that. She knew that what courage she possessed was weakening with every hour that passed, like the bars that showed the strength of the battery charge in the phone itself had diminished then disappeared. Even more than the highway she needed a place where she could recharge the phone.

That meant a town. A village probably wouldn't do: many did not have electricity.

Once they had scaled the hill slope on the north side of the river and had a clear path to follow, Malini called a halt. She wanted to study Kandan's maps. She sat cross-legged with one map on her lap and another two spread beside her. Banni, Nanda and the boys hung over her shoulders and offered unhelpful advice.

At first, the military maps baffled her. There were no labels, only numbers. Eventually she worked out that if a number began with a certain numeral it represented a type of structure, such as a bridge, or a checkpoint on the highway. Other numerals must signify towns.

With the river behind her, her best guess was that she was well within North Central Province. If they continued to head due west by the sun, they should reach the big highway after a further few kilometres. There appeared to be a town ahead where the river they had crossed passed under a highway bridge. Malini decided that was the town they would travel to in order to recharge the phone.

The first sign that Malini's calculations were right came when a helicopter with government markings broke into the sky from the south-west. Malini rushed the children off the track and into the dense cover of the forest. Through the foliage, she could see that the helicopter was keeping a course along a north-east line. It almost disappeared, but then returned, now on a south-west course. Malini guessed that it was scanning the highway below, flying up and down it. It was certainly not looking for them, but the helicopter pilot might radio down to a patrol if they were spotted.

Amal pointed a stick at the helicopter and pretended to blast it out of the sky.

The helicopter had gone out of sight and stayed out of sight for five minutes when Banni suddenly pricked up her ears and said, 'Someone is near.'

Malini said, 'It must be an animal.'

Banni said, 'A person.'

Nanda, whose nerves were more raw than Malini had realised, pulled the boys to her and squeezed her eyes shut, as if closed eyes made her invisible.

'Mama, is it soldiers?' Amal whispered.

Gayan said, 'Mama, I don't want soldiers. Mama, no soldiers.'

Banni listened for another few minutes, then declared that the person, whoever it was, had gone.

Malini led the children in the direction of the big highway, instructing Banni to listen for any sign of the helicopter's return, or for cars and trucks. 'We will hear the highway before we see it,' she said.

They reached the highway in the late afternoon. On each side of the asphalt the forest had been cut back a long way; it was not possible to cross without breaking cover and walking in clear view. They would have to wait until night. Malini and the children watched the traffic on the road from the fringe of the forest, counting five vehicles each minute heading south-west, and ten vehicles each minute heading north-east to Trincomalee. No cars were heading north-east, where the fighting was, only trucks carrying government soldiers and heavy weapons.

As Malini studied her maps, she realised that the town on the highway must lie further to the south. She could make out an elevated water tower further up the highway and she had to gamble that its symbol was the triple numeral on the map. A town inland from the north-east coast would probably be Tamil, since this was still a region more Tamil than Sinhalese, but at this stage of the war, it would be full of government soldiers. She decided that she would go alone to the town under cover of darkness. Then she would steal into a house with electricity lines attached, find a power point, plug in her mobile and recharge the battery for as long as she dared.

When she told the other children what she intended to do, the boys wept.

'What is wrong with you?' she asked them, and Amal, whose affection for Malini was always bubbling over, said, 'They will kill you!'

'No. I will be very careful.'

'They will put you into prison!'

Nanda whispered fretfully into Malini's ear. 'Malini, this is too dangerous. The boys and I will have to hide in the forest again if you are taken from us. That is why they are afraid. And...'

'And what?' said Malini.

'Pardon me for saying this, but your plan is mad.'

'Mad?' Malini felt herself plunging towards rage. 'Mad? I want to speak to my father. Is that mad? I have all of you to worry about every minute I am awake, but who takes care of me?'

Nanda recoiled as if she'd been slapped. 'I'm sorry, Malini.'

'I have become the slave of all of you,' said Malini. 'I am tired of it!'

And she stormed off, back along the track that had brought them all to the highway.

'Leave me be!' she shouted over her shoulder.

Nanda wept. 'Oh, what have I done?'

Banni put her arms around her. 'She is coming back, be sure of that. I will fix it.'

Amal and Gayan, their faces wet with tears, mimicked Nanda. '"What have I done? What have I done?"'

Banni comforted them. 'Don't cry, you silly things. Do you think Malini could leave you behind? Never in this world!'

Banni went off to find her sister.

She found Malini sitting cross-legged under a tree staring grimly ahead.

'Sister?'

'Go away!'

'Sister, may I sit with you for a short time?'

Banni attempted to take Malini's hand.

'No,' said Malini, and wrenched her hand away. 'Ennai thodaathe, don't touch me!'

'You miss Appa and Amma. That's the trouble.'

109

'Well, that is brilliantly perceptive of you! You should enrol in university immediately. The professors will be astounded.'

'I don't understand big words, Sister.'

'Then go away!'

'Sister, I want to speak about your plan.'

Malini, even in her anger and unhappiness, had to concede that her plan was a little desperate. But she was not about to admit that to her irritating sister.

'Go on, then.'

'Sister, you can't creep into a house and recharge the battery. You would have to stay hidden for an hour, or even more. In the first place, you would make a noise like an elephant. No, no, wait, Sister! You don't know how to creep. I'm sorry, but it is true. And you wouldn't do it anyway. Sister, you are a goody-two-shoes. You would...'

Malini said, 'I am a what?'

'A goody-two-shoes. I heard it on *The Simpsons*. Bart said Lisa is a goody-two-shoes. It means that—'

'I know what it means,' said Malini, smiling for the first time that day.

Banni was now sitting beside Malini, and had taken her hand to hold, acting as if she were the older sister. 'I have another idea. It's a big town we are looking for, isn't it? Only you and I will go. No one will know us. We must find a cheap guesthouse – we have enough money left. In our room there will be a place where we can plug in the phone. When the battery is charged, we will leave.'

Malini had been hoping that Banni's plan would be so ridiculous that she could laugh it to scorn. But in fact, it was clever. Apart from one or two things...

'We have no identity papers,' said Malini. 'We cannot register at a guesthouse, even a cheap one, without papers. And they will not accept us without a parent. And what if government soldiers stop us? Without papers they will lock us up.'

'We will slip past the soldiers. And we will tell the people at the guesthouse that you are my mother.'

'Do I look old enough to be your mother? You must spend the whole day dreaming up ways to insult me!'

'Keep your scarf over your face and speak in a bossy way. Say, "Banni, stand up straight! Banni, mind your manners!" Like that. You are tall. They will believe us.'

'I will think about it. "Mind your manners."'

Malini had to concede that her little sister was beginning to grow up. It was not just the common sense of her guesthouse idea; small actions had revealed that in the space of a few days, she had begun to shrug off her spoilt ways. Malini thought, *Underneath, she is stronger than me.*

Malini rejoined Nanda, Amal and Gayan to tell them of Banni's plan. Amal said, 'Aiee! Now they will kill you!' Then he spat on the ground and stamped on his spittle to destroy the power of a bad thought.

'No,' said Malini. 'I will come back and kiss you on your cheek. Then you will have a beautiful sleep and in the morning, a good breakfast.'

Chapter 12

Nanda, Amal and Gayan were to wait in the cover of the forest. 'But make sure you can still see the road,' Malini told Nanda. 'If government soldiers leave the road and start searching the bush for any reason, go deeper into the forest. Banni and I will come back to this place. If you are not here, we will wait. Whatever happens, Nanda, stay calm. If we do not come back in two days, continue the journey without us. Try to find the village of Ulla Alakana. Ask for my grandfather. I have written his name on this piece of paper. I have written a message, too. It says, *Care for Nanda, for Amal and Gayan as if they were part of our family.* I will leave the maps with you. See where I made this cross? That is where we are now. Head west.'

As Malini explained, almost in a whisper, Nanda nodded her head rapidly in agreement. Nanda's hands were trembling. She knew better than Malini what soldiers were capable of, both the SLA and the Tigers. Each night, she would wake at the slightest sound with her heart racing. At the orphanage, one of the soldiers without uniforms had held her by the hair while another soldier had pushed Master onto the ground and fired at him where he lay. He had kept firing even after he knew Master was dead. Nanda had not told Malini what she had been forced to watch.

Hiding in the forest after the massacre at the orphanage, she had been waiting for the blow that would kill her. Where it would come from she didn't know, but it would kill her. Instead, through a curtain of rain, she had glimpsed Malini beneath a satinwood tree. If Malini and Banni were taken by the soldiers, Nanda would not go on to the village of Ulla Alakana. She would remain where she was with the boys, and die.

Malini and Banni left for the town when it was dark, keeping to the fringe of the forest but within sight of the highway. Just as it had been during the day, most of the traffic was heading north towards the coast. When the trucks roared past with SLA soldiers in the back, Malini and Banni crouched down low and barely drew a breath. The soldiers were singing at the tops of their voices. They knew that their side was about to claim victory. Malini grieved to hear the singing, as if the war had been nothing but a huge party with fireworks and games and prizes for the winner.

Malini saw the silhouette of buildings in the distance, but very few lights. She told Banni, 'If we meet anyone, I will talk.' A dirt road branched off the highway close to the town, with the houses of small landholders on both sides. The symbols above the doorways of Hindu deities showed that this was a Tamil part of the town. The houses were all unlit, as if the residents wanted to keep to themselves, to hide.

The sisters walked quickly, with their heads bowed. Some sort of noisy gathering was taking place in the centre of the town, perhaps a victory celebration. They came to the market, but it was dark and deserted, the stalls all locked up. In a town of this size, a night market would normally stay open until eleven. In the centre of the market a Hindu shrine stood beneath a tree, but the figure of Shiva was not draped with garlands of flowers, as it should be.

An old Tamil woman came shuffling through the deserted market with a basket of bay leaves on her back, but she didn't greet them. Then they saw a sadhu on the other side of the market, standing as still as a statue with his staff in his hand. His white beard reached down to his waist. Malini approached him, hoping to ask if a guesthouse was nearby. It was only when she was right in from of him with her hands clasped that she saw tears running down his cheeks. He did not seem to see her; his gaze fixed on some place far away.

She said, 'I honour you, sir,' and left him to his grief.

Malini and Banni skirted the noisy celebration in the middle of the town and hurried along the empty streets, always staying in the shadows. Down one narrow lane that led back to the celebration, Malini glimpsed soldiers with their arms around each other's shoulders, heads raised to the stars as they bellowed out the words of what Malini recognised as a football song.

Now they were in a ghost town. Not a person to be seen, the only sounds the distant bellowing of the soldiers and occasional volleys of gunfire from the middle of town. They hurried past Tamil shops with their metal roller doors closed and padlocked. Banni saw a sign with an arrow pointing towards the Golden Sunshine Magnificent Guesthouse. When they found the guesthouse – a ramshackle building with a balcony on the first level – it looked anything but golden and magnificent. A small light burned in the office.

Malini pulled her scarf further forward, so that her face was in shadow. She mounted the three steps to the lobby with Banni, pushed against the door and found it locked. Malini tapped on the glass pane of the door, hoping to attract the attention of a man asleep at the reception desk.

The tapping didn't rouse him.

She found a pull cord and tugged at the handle. A bell sounded inside, but still the man remained asleep.

She tugged again and again. Finally the man awoke. He rubbed his face with his hands, yawned mightily, then shuffled to the door.

'Go away,' he said. 'Curfew!'

'Please,' said Malini. 'Do you have any rooms?'

The man pulled down a blind on his side of the door.

'Please, sir, we have money to pay,' Malini called. His departing footsteps announced the ruin of their plan.

Malini searched in vain down every dark street they could find for a guesthouse that would admit them. Malini wasn't able to find anyone who would even speak to her. As tiredness and despair set in, they lost their way. They rounded a corner from a lane and walked straight into a patrol of two government soldiers. Both soldiers lifted their rifles and pointed them at Malini and Banni.

'We are on our way home,' Malini said, in Sinhala. Her voice was steady, despite her dread.

'This little fool speaks our tongue,' one soldier said. A pink birthmark shaped like a banana reached from the corner of his left eye down to his upper lip. 'Where did you learn Sinhala, little fool?'

'In my school, sir,' said Malini.

'Don't give me that,' the soldier said. 'What Tamil school would teach Sinhala? I think you're a liar, little fool. You are a liar, aren't you?'

The other soldier had stepped forward and was feeling the silk of Malini's scarf between his fingers. She pushed his hand away.

'Please may we go?' she said.

'Oh, you can go all right,' said the first soldier. 'It's just a matter of where you go.'

He reached out and felt Malini's hair. He may have had something more to say, something cruel and clever, except that Banni grabbed his hand from her sister's hair and bit down hard. The soldier screamed; Banni held on like a bulldog. Malini swung her elbow into the stomach of the second soldier, and by good fortune caught him so unaware – he may also have been drunk – that he doubled over. Malini grabbed a handful of Banni's blouse, wrenched her free and together they raced back down the lane. Malini heard the rapid chatter of a rifle and the whining echo of bullets, but she kept running, only just keeping up with Banni. They had no plan; they simply turned whenever they came to an intersection. Malini couldn't tell if the soldiers were still following. She stopped to listen and heard nothing, but Banni cried out, 'There!' as the soldiers burst from an alley.

Malini shrieked and took off again, Banni beside her. Now they were in a cul-de-sac with two-storey houses rearing on either side, protected from the street by tall walls. The only way out was back in the direction of the soldiers. The sisters pressed themselves against a high wooden gate, hoping that they wouldn't be visible. At the mouth of the cul-de-sac they could see the soldiers deliberating. One called out, 'Where are you, little fool? We won't hurt you! We only want to cut your pretty throat!'

The soldiers advanced down the street, their rifles held at fire-ready positions. Malini whispered rapidly, 'Appa, Amma, please pardon me for failing you. Please, Lord Shiva, help us now if you love us.'

Suddenly the wooden gate swung open and a voice hissed, 'Come in! Be quick!'

Malini and Banni did what they were told. The gate closed behind them.

They were in a garden, the dark forms of trees rearing around them. A shadow in the shape of a girl – the source of the whisper – closed the gate quietly, then gestured for Malini and Banni to follow her up four steps to the veranda of a very grand house, then around to one side.

'Wait here,' said the girl. 'You will be safe. You have my promise.'

She vanished down a laneway that ran along the side of the house. Malini and Banni heard a door open and close. Then nothing for long minutes except the sound of music coming from inside the house, and the shouts of the two soldiers out on the street.

'Little fool, where are you? Don't worry, we will kill you quickly! You and that little tiger!'

'Is this a trap?' Banni whispered.

Malini said, 'I don't think so. She could have left us to the soldiers if she'd wished to.'

'Did you see me bite banana face?'

'Shush, now.'

The girl returned, carrying what looked like textbooks. Malini noticed that she wore glasses. The girl held a finger to her lips. 'Just follow,' she said. 'Say nothing.'

Malini and Banni kept close to the girl as they crept up the laneway to a garden at the rear of the house.

The girl motioned for Malini and Banni to wait while she opened the door to a small bungalow with a key. She stepped inside, beckoned to the sisters, then closed the door behind them. The girl then struck a match and lit an oil lamp, adjusting the flame carefully until it burned low.

In the golden glow of the lamp, the girl was fully revealed for the first time. Malini thought she looked around her own age, with long hair taken up on top and held loosely with a clasp. She wore stylish slacks and a cream-coloured blouse that may have been silk. Her glasses had narrow black frames and gave her a scholarly look, but she was also very assured and charming. She was the loveliest girl that Malini had ever seen, and in her grubby sari Malini felt as if she'd crawled out of a drainpipe.

The girl gestured, inviting them to sit on the rug-covered sofa along one wall. 'Please.'

She herself sat on a four-legged stool with a rush seat, facing the sisters. The textbooks she had brought with her sat on the floor beside the stool. 'Will I speak Tamil?' she asked, in Tamil.

'Or Sinhala,' said Malini, 'or English.'

'Really?'

Malini wanted to say, 'I am educated,' but she kept quiet.

'I am Randevee,' the girl said in English. 'I am sorry for your ordeal. The soldiers are barbarians. Will you drink some guava juice? I have some here.'

Malini said, 'Thank you. That would be very

welcome.' She was trying to sound as courteous as she possibly could.

While Randevee poured juice from a decanter into two tall glasses, Banni asked Malini in a whisper what a barbarian was.

Malini whispered back, 'A wild person. Like you.'

'I was in the garden when I heard the soldiers chasing you,' said Randevee. She leaned forward on the stool as she spoke, clasped hands resting on her knees. 'I heard you scream.'

'It was our good fortune to meet you, Miss Randevee,' said Malini. 'I am Malini, and this is my sister, Banni.'

Banni glanced up at her sister to see if she should say anything. Malini nodded.

'Very pleased meeting you today,' Banni said in English, not getting it quite right.

'We are not from the town,' said Malini. 'We are from far off, close to the coast.'

'And how is it that you are here in this dangerous place? This town is half Sinhalese, half Tamil. But it is only your Tamil people who are suffering now.'

Malini had every reason to feel she could trust Randevee, and yet she had to overcome a stubborn reluctance to speak openly and honestly with a Sinhalese. It had been different with Nanda and the boys – they had come into her life in a way that made it impossible to think of them as anything other than victims. But Randevee lived a privileged life, to judge from the big house, her stylish clothing and her poise, and age-old enmities that Malini did not even believe in – that she hated, in fact – made her pause before she spoke up.

Randevee seemed to notice Malini's wariness. She said, 'But first, shall I tell you about myself?' She was home from school in Colombo for term break. Her parents had wanted her to stay away from the town during this dreadful time, but she had insisted on coming home.

'My father owns tourist resorts all over Sri Lanka,' she said. 'Ten altogether. One in the hills close to us here. And we have three houses in Sri Lanka, counting this one.' Randevee gestured towards the huge house. 'But this is my father's favourite because he came from this town when he was young and poor. I have two brothers, much older than me. One in Colombo, one in India. They are both businessmen. I am sorry to say that I argue with my father all the time. I tell him, *We have too much. It is wrong.* He supports the government and thinks the war is necessary. Did you hear the music in the house? My father is holding a party to celebrate the victory of the government. I will tell you what I think of the war. It is a disaster for our country. A horrible disaster.'

Malini agreed. 'I think so, too.'

'Do you know what I was doing in the garden? I was looking at the stars and thinking, up there is beauty, but down here is ugliness. When I go to university, I want to do something that will bring beauty back to our island. I'm going to be a doctor. I will go where the poor people are and give them free medicine.'

This sounded a bit pie-in-the-sky to Malini – she wondered whether Randevee had ever actually met any 'poor people'. But what she felt even more strongly was something like envy. To go to university – that was Malini's great dream.

'To Colombo University?' said Malini.

'Oh, no,' said Randevee. 'To Cambridge University in England. My name is down in the Department of Medicine.'

Malini closed her eyes for a moment as a wave of longing swept over her. Cambridge University! She had seen pictures of the famous colleges in books. Oh, if she could go to Cambridge and study mathematics, that would be paradise. But Cambridge, or any university, was so far in the future, further than ever, and Malini, with a great effort of will, shut her mind to such daydreams. She said softly to Randevee, 'How lucky you are.'

Then Randevee said, 'If you are not from around here, where are you from? And what has brought you to my town, if I may ask?'

Malini was unsure how much she should tell Randevee. The girl's eyes were so clear, her gaze so candid, but there was something else there, too: something that Malini could not quite grasp.

Nevertheless, she told Randevee everything, from her escape with Banni into the forest, to meeting Nanda and the boys, the encounter with Kandan, and of course, their destination: the village of Ulla Alakana.

'I have not heard of Ulla Alakana,' said Randevee. 'It must be far.'

Malini said, 'Not too far, I hope.' Then she said, 'Randevee, when we parted from my father, he gave me his mobile phone so that we might make contact. But I must recharge the battery. Is it possible I could do that here?'

'Certainly,' said Randevee. 'But I must tell you, Malini, that the mobile signal here disappears for days at a time.' And she added, in English, 'Alas.'

Malini had been keeping one eye on an electrical socket in the wall behind Randevee even while she told her story, and now she slipped the mobile and the recharger from inside her sari and quickly attached them to the power source. She waited for the blank screen to register that the phone was charging, then with great relief resumed her seat on the sofa.

Banni whispered, 'Two people are coming. Men.'

Randevee said, 'Don't worry.'

She opened one of the textbooks she'd brought with her, and when a knock came at the door, calmly stood and called, in Sinhala, 'Who is it?'

A voice called back, 'Security, miss.'

Malini flinched; Banni, as if preparing for a fight, lifted two small fists.

Randevee opened the door just a little. 'What is your business?' she asked.

'Your father wants you in the house,' a man's voice replied. A second voice added, 'Tamil devils are making trouble in the town.'

'I am doing homework,' said Randevee. 'I need peace and quiet.'

'You must come now, miss.'

'I will come in a minute. Go your way.'

She closed the door. They heard the security men departing, after some hesitation.

'I will go, then come back,' said Randevee. 'I'll be half an hour. You stay here.' She took Malini's hand. Her face was glowing with excitement. 'Don't be afraid,' she said. 'By good fortune, you have come to the right place.'

Malini and Banni spent the first fifteen minutes before Randevee's return crouched over the mobile phone, watching the recharge light flashing. 'Imagine, Banni,' whispered Malini, 'a little longer and the phone will be charged. Then when we find a signal, maybe there will be a call or a message from Appa!'

'I'll speak to him first,' said Banni, 'and to Amma. I won't tell them you've been bossy, don't worry.'

'So kind of you,' said Malini.

The sisters looked around the bungalow. It appeared to be accommodation for guests. There was a pile of folded white towels in the bathroom. Everything was spotlessly clean and fresh. Malini looked longingly at the double bed with its big plush pillows, thinking of the luxury of a few minutes' comfortable rest. The tall space-age refrigerator in the kitchen was twice the size of the one in Malini's house. A painting of the Buddha sitting cross-legged beneath his Bodhi tree hung on a wall in the living room. The Buddha held up one hand with the palm facing out – a gesture of peace. A small statuette of Dancing Krishna sat on a sideboard nearby. It was not uncommon for households in this region to display both Buddhist and Hindu icons, as Malini knew. In times past, the two faiths had often enjoyed each other's company. But almost all households had opted for displaying the symbols of just one faith during the years of civil war. Why not in this household, Malini wondered, when Randevee's father so strongly supported the government side?

Randevee returned after half an hour, struggling into the bungalow with a red suitcase. She closed the door behind her, listened for a minute, then swung the suitcase up onto the sofa. 'I have everything here!' she said. She was in a state of high excitement, almost gleeful. She opened the two clasps that kept the suitcase shut and displayed the contents.

'I have some dresses for you,' she said, holding one of them up for Malini and Banni to see, an expensive-looking garment of pink and green chiffon that might be worn to a party. 'I have some slacks for you, too. Three pairs. They will be the right size for you, Malini – they're too small for me now. And some shoes. Also two jackets, in case you go somewhere nice.'

She didn't mention the lacy undergarments in a variety of colours, but they were in clear view. 'And this beret,' she said, handing Malini a stylish red felt cap, 'for when you're just walking along.'

Banni looked at Malini and made a face, a comical grimace, without Randevee noticing. It was the sort of face people put on when they mean, 'Totally nuts!'

'Randevee,' said Malini, holding the red beret, 'what is all this?'

'For you to keep. For your journey.'

'Randevee, it is very kind of you, but—'

'No – you must take all this, Malini! Please.'

'The most valuable thing to us was the opportunity to charge our mobile phone, Randevee. For that we cannot thank you enough. And for saving our lives. But I'm afraid I will have no opportunity to wear your lovely dresses.'

Randevee slumped onto the sofa. When she finally spoke, her voice was a squeak. 'I am so bored in Colombo. And I'm bored here. You have adventures every day, and I have nothing but silly parties and shopping with my mother. I want my life to be real, like yours.'

Malini sighed. Only a short time ago, Randevee had made her feel so unsophisticated, and now she felt about a hundred years older than her, and a great deal wiser.

Randevee looked at Malini. 'My heart is full of sympathy for your Tamil people,' she said. 'I am not a bigot – please don't believe that, Malini! See how I have placed a statue of Krishna here? When my father says, *Crush the rebels*, I become sick in my stomach. I wish I could come with you. That's what I wish.'

Malini was moved, but not past reason.

'Randevee,' she said, 'this is not an adventure. This is life and death to us. We have been travelling for five days. I feel tired and dirty and all I do is worry. If I could trade my life for a boring one with my father and mother close by again, I would do it in an instant. Your kindness to Banni and to me has been a great gift. But you should not wish to be with us. We may all be dead in an hour or a day or a week.'

Randevee sat with her head bowed. Banni stood beside her with one hand resting on her back. She whispered into Randevee's ear, in the best English she could muster, 'She is a big bossy. But she is right.'

Chapter 13

Nanda and the boys were patient, but when they heard the distant sound of gunfire, Gayan became frantic. Nanda folded him in her arms. 'Be calm,' she said. His heart was beating as rapidly as a cat's. Since the destruction of the orphanage, something as small as the sudden snapping of a twig in a forest could send him into a frenzy. On that day of fire and murder he'd seen shocking things, and he couldn't ever forget them.

Nanda whispered prayers into Gayan's ear, and urged him to join in, but when the prayer was finished, he said, 'They will kill Malini. They will kill Banni.'

'No, Gayan,' said Nanda. 'They will not.' That's what she said, but it was not what she believed. She thought that they would never see Malini and Banni again.

Amal said, 'If those devils kill Malini and Banni, I will kill them.'

'Amal!' Nanda was horrified.

'Am I a coward?' said Amal. 'No. I will find a gun and go to the town and kill them all! I hate the soldiers. I hate the red hats. I hate the tiger stripes.'

Nanda thrust Gayan aside, seized Amal and slapped his face, hard. 'Listen to me! None of that! None of it!'

Amal felt his cheek. He thrust his chin defiantly at Nanda. 'I am not a coward!' he said. Then he relented. 'Sorry.'

A new volley of gunfire rang out from the town. Gayan shrieked and jumped to his feet. He covered his ears with his hands. Nanda reached for him, but he avoided her and ran headlong across the cleared area towards the highway. Nanda called to him but he didn't stop. She hissed at Amal, 'Stay here!' and followed.

Gayan had chosen a bad time to give way to panic. An open truck with a half-dozen soldiers in the back was heading down the highway, and Gayan froze in its path. The driver braked hard; the soldiers in the back were flung forward. Gayan stood in the glare of the headlights, his mouth wide open in a silent scream. The driver stuck his head out the window, hurling abuse at the child. Nanda, forgetting her fear of guns, rushed up to Gayan and flung her arms around him. Three soldiers jumped down from the back of the truck. One strode up to Nanda and struck her on the side of the head. Another seized Gayan by his hair and threw him full length along the surface of the road.

'Idiot!' he shouted at the boy.

'What are they?' the driver called to the soldiers. 'Human or devils?'

One Sri Lankan can usually tell if another Sri Lankan is Sinhalese or Tamil at a glance, but Nanda in her oversized Bon Jovi T-shirt and Gayan in his pyjamas mystified the soldiers. One of the soldiers leaned over Nanda and thrust his fist under her nose.

'If you understand me, insect, speak up,' he said in Sinhala.

Nanda, in her terror, babbled something that could have been Sinhala or Swahili or any language on earth.

The soldier grasped her throat and lifted her off the ground. 'She's having trouble speaking,' he said, to the amusement of all the soldiers, those standing with him and those still in the truck. 'Say something, insect!'

Then, 'What ho! What ho, I say!' Out of the darkness of the night, a figure emerged – maybe a boy, maybe a man – dancing on the highway in a weird, jerky manner, like a puppet. The figure made a blubbering sound with his lips, leaping about and waving his arms. The soldier holding Nanda dropped her and swung his automatic rifle down from his shoulder. Before he could fire, the figure was gone. But the voice still called out shrilly, in English, 'What ho! Pardon me!'

More soldiers leapt down from the truck, everybody shouting at the one time. In the confusion, Nanda gestured to Gayan and both crept under the truck, out the other side, and into the darkness. Nanda crouched low, her arm around Gayan's shoulders. She could hear the soldiers shouting and, every so often, the mysterious chirrup of the voice calling, 'What ho! Pardon me!'

Shots were fired. It took some time for the shouting of the soldiers to die down and a few more minutes before the truck engine roared to life. Nanda raised her head to watch the tail-lights of the vehicle grow dimmer and dimmer.

They made their way back to Amal and the carry bags at the fringe of the forest. Once they were all together again, Nanda said what soothing words she could find to Amal, who was trembling after hearing the guns, then she excused herself, crawled a short distance away from the boys, and threw up. She began to shake uncontrollably, a fit brought on by dread. She saw in her mind's eye the broad face of the soldier who had held her by the throat, the hatred in his eyes. When the shaking died down, she lifted the fringe of her Bon Jovi T-shirt and bit down hard on the fabric to stop herself from screaming.

A voice whispered, 'Nanda!' and she dropped the hem of the T-shirt and glanced around in a renewed bout of panic.

In the moonlight she could make out the huge white smile on the face of Kandan.

She stared at him without properly understanding anything, except that he was no longer wearing the sling on his arm.

'Nanda, it's me,' whispered Kandan, in Sinhala. Then in English, 'What ho! What ho! Pardon me!'

Nanda threw her arms around his neck. She was still holding tight when Kandan first sank to his knees, then toppled onto his back.

'What's wrong?' she said.

Gayan and Amal had now joined them.

Kandan said, 'Nothing.' Then, on his back in the moonlight, he opened his shirt. 'Only this.'

Blood glittered. A wound in his side below his heart had turned his shirt black. Nanda raised her hands to her face in horror. Life was ebbing from his body. And yet his smile remained.

'What ho,' he murmured. 'What ho…'

Chapter 14

Randevee, crestfallen, left Malini and Banni alone in the bungalow while the phone battery finished charging, but returned later in pyjamas and dressing gown. She asked Malini to accept three American twenty-dollar notes and a bag of food from the kitchen, which included many leftover cakes, sandwiches and vol-au-vents from the party. A second bag included some of the clothing from the suitcase she'd offered Malini earlier. She said, 'May you prosper on your journey.'

She led Malini and Banni to a gate at the back of the garden and unlocked it with a long-barrelled key. 'To the left, then to the left again,' she said. 'You will find the highway. Then you turn right.'

Malini was about to say farewell, but Randevee shook her head. The light of a lantern above the gate showed the glitter of tears in her eyes.

She accepted Malini's kiss on the cheek. 'Write me a letter or call me,' she said. 'Both would be better.' She had entered her address in Colombo and her phone number in the contacts file on Malini's phone.

The gate closed.

Malini and Banni hurried down a lane, turned left into a broader street, and as Randevee had promised, came to the big highway. They kept to the verge, ducking down into the grass whenever a vehicle approached.

They had to find the right place to turn from the highway and cut across the tall grass to where Nanda and the boys were waiting. Malini hadn't thought to leave a marker on the roadside. She stopped and glanced back the way she had come, then ahead, then back again.

'I don't know where they are,' she confessed to her sister.

Banni closed her eyes and lifted her head. 'Keep going,' she said. Every hundred paces, Banni stopped and listened in her strange way, as if she were an animal, searching for a scent on the night breeze. After a number of these stops, she said, 'Wait!' She turned her head around and about, then her lips curled upward in a smile, for she had heard a young boy's voice.

Nanda, Amal and Gayan rushed out of their hiding place to meet Banni and Malini. The boys threw themselves at Malini. Nanda kissed Malini again and again. Then came a scream.

It was Banni. She was standing a few metres away. Malini pushed the boys aside.

'Banni, what is it?'

Banni had fallen to her knees, her head thrown back, a long howl rising towards the moon and stars.

Nanda and the boys said nothing.

Malini took two steps and found herself gazing down at Kandan, his body straight and still, his arms at his side. His eyes were closed.

Nanda told the story. Malini didn't speak a word, didn't ask any questions. When Nanda had finished, Malini said, 'He is to be buried.'

With the short-bladed knife, with sticks and bare hands, Malini, Banni, Nanda, Amal and Gayan dug a grave at a place where the soil was free of tree roots; they dug steadily, almost without talking, for two hours. Then Malini spoke Tamil prayers and threw the first handfuls of earth onto Kandan's body, his face covered with Nanda's bloodstained shirt. Nanda, Banni and the two boys pushed more earth over the edge of the grave, and more earth and more, until it was full and the soil began to form a small mound. Amal sang a sutra of farewell. Banni wept without ceasing for the whole of the burial. Such a short time any of them had known Kandan, and yet his death reached deep into each of them. Gayan, at the graveside, weaved his head from side to side in grief and tapped his chest above his heart with his hand in a constant motion.

Malini's own grief took the form of silence. She should have allowed Kandan to come with them. It was wrong to make him stay behind, even if she had her reasons. And she thought, too, that the boy was not meant for war, with his silly jokes and his ceaseless chatter and his smile and laughter. He had escaped the war and found a home with this family of refugees, and now that family was burying him.

It was important that they cross the highway under cover of darkness. Malini distributed cakes and sandwiches, allowed everyone a tiny sip of Pepsi, then led the way, Malini herself in her worn sari; Nanda in a rainbow blouse of Randevee's; Banni in her green blouse; the boys in their Bart Simpson pyjamas.

The cleared area on the far side of the highway was not broad. Malini and her family slipped into the forest safely and found shelter beneath the boughs of a fallen tree. Only two hours or so remained before dawn. Malini said, 'Sleep, if you can. If you can't sleep, at least rest your hearts.' The two boys settled together; Malini, Banni and Nanda found a grassy spot of their own. But before long, Gayan and Amal came and snuggled down with the girls. Malini knew that allowing the boys to sleep next to them would be breaking the strict rules of both their faiths, but they had recently buried their friend, and Malini was happy to give what comfort she could.

As soon as the boys were asleep, Malini roused Banni, told Nanda they would be back shortly, and crept with her sister to the fringe of the forest.

The phone played 'Greensleeves' when Malini

turned it on. A red logo appeared on the screen, depicting the head of an eagle, and the three letters from the English alphabet that identified the service provider. So far, so good.

Then the screen image changed – a picture of Malini herself as a child of five with a mouthful of white teeth seated on her father's shoulders – Appa's favourite photo of her. Tears rushed into Malini's eyes.

The gauge showed that the phone was receiving a weak signal. Malini crept closer to the highway, Banni following, and the signal strengthened. A message jumped onto the screen: twenty-seven missed calls, two messages. Malini squealed.

Banni said, 'Show me! Show me!'

But a password was required before Malini could access the messages.

'Banni, do you remember the password?'

'I've forgotten.'

Malini ransacked her memory, searching for the word. It was an English word, she remembered, not Tamil, not Sinhalese.

'It's to do with food,' said Malini, pressing her fingers against her forehead.

'I remember!'

'What?'

'Banana.'

'It's not banana.'

Something came to Malini. 'It's what Appa called me when I was little and chubby.'

'What's that got to do with food?'

137

'Pudding! He called me pudding.'

The missed calls dated back three days. The two messages were identical and very brief. 'Call us back on this number when you can. Our love.'

Malini dialled with her heart in her mouth. There was no answer. She dialled again, and again – no answer. She waited for five minutes in a fever of longing, then dialled again. No answer.

She left a message: 'Call me!'

They waited.

Banni yawned. Despite her yearning to talk to her mother and father, her eyelids were growing heavy. 'Wake me when Appa and Amma answer,' she said. She was asleep in seconds, her head in Malini's lap. Malini, herself aching with fatigue, sat with the phone in one hand, the other hand resting on her sister's head. The first, faint light of dawn was turning the eastern sky a pale grey.

In her trance of weariness, memories drifted back to Malini like boats appearing on the horizon, one after another. She saw her father tying mango and margosa leaves around the door of the house to celebrate her results in a national maths competition – equal first in the whole of Sri Lanka. The custom of ornamenting the door with leaves on special days did not usually include coming first in maths competitions, but her father couldn't contain his delight. 'My little pudding has a brain as big as the moon!' he'd said, which

138

was a bit embarrassing, because she was no longer a 'pudding'. Another golden memory was of bathing in the river with her mother and other girls and women of the town at the end of fasting, just six months ago. She had bathed with her mother many times before, but this time all the mothers fussed over her. They spoke to her as if she were no longer a child but a young woman, and came close to whisper to her. 'Such beautiful hair I have never seen!' And, 'The soft skin of a queen!' Malini had known that these were ritual words of praise that would be bestowed on any girl who had turned fourteen, but they still gave her pleasure.

She remembered, too, the long hours she'd spent with her mother in the kitchen, learning the thousand rules of food preparation in a Tamil household: what was to be served on certain days; what foods must never be served on the one plate; the ritual and ceremonial properties of every herb and spice in the round world; who was to be allowed to fill his dish first at big gatherings (it was always a 'he'); who came second, third, fourth, all the way down to one hundredth, and beyond. Oh, and that day – actually many days! – when her father and mother argued over what their daughters should hold sacred when it came to caste. Malini's father did not honour caste as well as he might, and refused to speak of his own caste, Vellalar, as more important than any other caste. Malini's mother always returned to the one point: 'Face reality, Kanavar!' And Malini saw a filmy image of her father calmly making the point *he* always returned to: 'Malini's caste is Genius. Banni's caste is Precious Princess. There, I am done with it.'

Malini's head was drooping low over the sleeping form of her sister when the phone rang, playing the tune of 'Beat It', chosen by Banni some months earlier. Malini was wide awake in an instant, sitting upright so abruptly that Banni was flung from her lap.

'Hello! Appa, is it you?'

'It is me, my love. Such joy, to hear your voice!'

'Appa! Oh, Appa! Is Amma with you?'

'She is here. And Banni?'

'Banni is safe here with me, Appa.'

'Let your mother hear your voices.'

Malini handed the phone to Banni. She said, 'Amma? I want to go home, Amma!'

Over the phone came wailing, interrupted by the girls' names being repeated rapidly. Then, 'I bless all the gods of the world for your safety!'

Malini allowed her sister to talk to their mother and father for more than a minute – enough time for Banni to mention a few issues she had with being bossed about and to tell her father that their friend Kandan had died. She was about to tell him more about Kandan, but her father said, 'For your friend, I am sorry. But now, give the phone to Malini.'

'I'm here, Appa.'

'Tell me your situation.'

'Appa, we are walking to find Appappa. We have come a long way. I think we are close now. We have crossed the great highway below the big reservoir at

Kantale, I think. If we head west, we will pass north of Galenbindunuwewa and find Ulla Alakana. I hope.'

'Ah, beloved Daughter! Listen, I have little time left to talk. We are in some danger, I must not deceive you about that. Keep to your path. Daughter, you are so brave, my heart is full of pride. Now I must go.'

'Appa!'

'I must go, Daughter. If it is possible, I will call again in three days.'

The call ended.

Such a storm of tears overcame Malini! She threw back her head and howled. She had heard the voices of her mother and father, which was ecstasy, and now the voices were gone. Banni tried to console her sister, but it was impossible. Then Nanda and the boys appeared, their expressions full of concern. They circled Malini and touched her face, her arms; they kissed her hands.

Then the storm passed, and Malini sat in silence, staring at the phone in her hand. Finally, she looked up and smiled and allowed Nanda to dry her tears with the hem of her blouse.

'What a baby I am!' said Malini. 'Forgive me, children. I have been speaking to Appa and Amma.'

Malini was silent again, for minute after minute. Then she said, 'We will eat something. After we eat, we return to our path.'

Malini sat with another of Kandan's maps on her knees and tried to work out the route they would take. What she had told her father was mostly based on guesses. The highway was clear on the map, but with only numbers and symbols to go by, she would have to feel her way to Ulla Alakana: further west was her best estimate, or perhaps slightly north-west. The time would come when she would be compelled to ask for directions.

They traipsed into the woodland once again. Strangely, the forest on the western side of the highway was not quite the same as the forest on the eastern side. There were many more tall trees. Nanda, who had spent time in orphanage camps surrounded by such trees, told the others their Sinhalese names – rata kekuna, bulu, telamba. The bulus, she said, had magic in them. If you rested beneath one and filled your mind with thoughts of the Buddha, forest animals would come to your feet and offer themselves for your cooking pot. Malini laughed at the story, but Nanda insisted, 'No, no, it is true!'

Within an hour, the tall trees thinned out and the ground became level. But then, an obstacle appeared: a very extensive swamp, reeds rising from it for as far as the eye could see.

Malini gazed at the swamp, wishing she had Kandan with her to walk out and test the depth. Wishing that Kandan was still alive. Wishing many things.

'I am going to see how high the water is,' she told Banni and Nanda. She handed the phone to Banni, took two steps, three steps, and on the fourth disappeared beneath the water. She surfaced again and struggled back to shore. Gayan and Amal were hooting with laughter.

Banni was staring at her in fascination and horror. 'Disgusting.'

Malini was about to demand exactly what was disgusting when she saw that her hands and arms were covered in leeches. Not the small brown leeches that everyone on the island had to deal with at some time, but fat black monsters, the size of slugs.

Malini stayed calm. Her father had taught her how to remove leeches.

'Give me the box of matches,' she said to Banni.

She lit one match after another, touching the flame to the leeches. Gayan and Amal were thrilled by the spectacle and asked to hold the burning matches. Malini denied them the delight they craved, but allowed Nanda to help. The task repulsed Nanda, but she persisted. At first, the heat of the flame made the leeches bite more deeply, but then they released their grip and dropped off, leaving a bleeding sore. The real danger of a leech bite was not the blood the leech took, but the wound it left, which could easily become infected. Once Malini had burned the leeches from her skin, she rubbed antiseptic powder into the bleeding bites. She said to herself, *When you next have an idea, Malini, I want you to store it carefully in your brain, and leave it there. Forever.*

It was difficult to tell whether it would be a shorter journey to skirt the swamp by heading south, or north.

In the end, Malini chose to go north, simply for the sake of moving on.

It wasn't long before they came upon an old man with his trousers rolled up. All the skin of his legs below his knees was dyed a blue as vivid as the sky. He was using a net attached to a very long bamboo pole to fish leeches from the swamp. On the shore was a large tin, once an engine oil container, its top now removed, and into this tin he dropped the leeches from his net.

Malini and the children watched the old man at work for a few minutes before he responded to their presence.

When he turned to face them they saw that he was blind, his eyes covered by pale cataracts. He spoke in Tamil. 'Far from home, wayfarers!'

'We are, sir,' said Malini. 'Sir, might you tell me if we must travel far to get around the swamp?'

'No rooster? Is the hen in charge of the chicken house?' said the old man, and he let out a cackling laugh. Then he said, 'You have questions. I can count them. Why are my old legs blue? It is a dye made of herbs that my leech brothers hate. Ha! Let them hate it! Why do I take my leech brothers from their home and put them in my tin? The doctors of our land buy them from me. It is no hardship for the leech brothers. The doctors pamper them and they feast each day on good thick blood. It is a wonder in the world that they do not jump into my net by themselves!'

Malini said, 'Sir, is it far from here to the end of the swamp? We wish to go west, but the swamp is in the way.'

144

'In the way?' said the old man. 'Ha! The swamp lived here before your appappa was born. In the way?'

Banni crept close and looked into the leech gatherer's tin. It seethed with the fat creatures, and she stepped back quickly.

The old man said, 'They frighten you, little one? Not every creature is beautiful.'

Malini tried again. 'Sir, my question?'

'Mrs Hen has a question! Do I have an answer for her? No, it is not far. Two days' walking, then you can go west.'

'Two days!'

'Two if you walk fast. Or three.'

'Sir, that's a long journey!'

'No, Mrs Hen. From here to the hot sun is a long journey. From here to Lord Shiva's bower at the centre of the universe is a long journey. Two days is nothing. Or three.'

Malini thanked the old man, as courtesy demanded, even though he'd left her feeling bleak. Two days or even three just to get back on a westward course!

A saying that Malini's father often muttered with a sigh went like this: *There are no corners in a round world.* What did he mean? That we shouldn't be looking for good fortune when we turn a corner, but accept what our eyes can see. Malini was repeating those words about corners and a round world to herself as she led her sister and Nanda and the boys along the fringe of the swamp. Her spirits were not so low now; as soon as she thought of the phone inside her sari, and of her father's promised call, she smiled. At the same time, she would have been very grateful for a corner; very grateful for some good fortune. And somehow, she found it, without any corners in sight.

From among the reeds that grew tallest here on the shore of the swamp emerged a man dressed in rubber boots that came up almost to his armpits. He wore a tightly bound red Tamil turban and grasped in each hand was a writhing eel. He said in Tamil, 'Adjuna the fisherman is my name to all. What names are you given?'

Malini rattled off names, steeling herself to stand her ground as the eels thrashed about in the fisherman's grip.

Adjuna the fisherman sloshed up onto the bank. 'Will you say hello?' he said, and thrust one of the eels towards Gayan, the most alarmed of the children. Gayan let out a shriek and hid himself behind Nanda. Then the man in the strange boots held the eel's head up to his own face. 'No friends here, meen!' he said to the fish. And with that, he lifted the eel to his mouth and bit down hard just behind the head, then did the same to the second eel. He threw both eels to the ground, where they wriggled for a few seconds before falling still.

Without knowing what she was doing, Malini had taken three or four steps backwards from both the man and the eels. They repulsed her, much more than the leeches, each a metre long and as thick as the fisherman's wrists. In death, their open mouths revealed rows of small glittering teeth. Was the swamp full of nothing but the most hideous creatures of the island?

Nanda, however, had crouched down and was prodding the eels with her finger. 'Fat fish,' she said in Sinhala. 'You will do well in the market, sir.'

'Don't touch them!' Banni shrieked. 'Are you mad?'

Nanda shrugged. 'I was sent to work in the Tamil fish market of Colombo when I was five,' she said. 'I gutted a hundred eels each week. The people who owned me told the market man I was Tamil. I have no fear of eels.'

And here was the good fortune: the fisherman in the rubber boots that saved him from leech bites, who gave his name as Adjuna, owned a boat, full of freshly killed eels, and told Malini that he would not see her walking for ages to skirt the swamp but would carry her and the children across. 'Sister,' he said, 'would Shiva forgive me if I made you walk, or swim? The eels would eat you.'

The boat, concealed in the reeds nearby, was long and narrow, designed to push its way through the reeds. It was forced through the water not by oars, but with a long pole.

More than one trip across the swamp would be needed to carry everyone in Malini's family to the far shore. She sent the boys and Nanda first, while she waited with Banni. The boys were thrilled to be in the boat, but seeing Malini left behind caused them to wail like frightened cats.

Malini called out to them, 'Be brave!'

The boys called back, 'Aiee! We will die in the water!'

Malini and Banni lay down in the grass to wait. They were both so tired from walking that they had forgotten the lesson they had learned as small children: Naga lives in the tall grass and Naga will rise up and strike you dead. Naga was the snake, the cobra, with his flared hood, eyes circled in black and fangs dripping with poison. And Naga was at this moment rearing above Malini and Banni where they lay with their eyes shut in the tall grass.

Banni opened her eyes first. She yawned, raised herself on one elbow, and froze.

This Naga was a monster of his tribe, very thick just below his neck and two metres long. His scales were a greyish colour, changing to bronze close to his head. On the back of his flared hood a strange design had been drawn by nature, as if he had eyes in the back of his head.

Naga was flicking his forked tongue rapidly, tasting the scent of human in the air. He weaved his head from side to side as if steadying himself for his lightning-fast thrust. Banni had seen a Naga like this attack a rat under the mango tree in the garden of her parents' house. The snake had sunk his fangs into the rat's head, holding on for minute after minute, coiling his body as the rat writhed and squealed. She had seen the rat finally grow still as the deadly venom spread through its veins.

This Naga was much bigger.

Banni whispered to Malini, 'Sister, Naga is here.'

Malini muttered, 'What?'

'Sister, Naga is here.'

Malini opened her eyes. She saw nothing for a moment, then her gaze settled on Naga. Her instinct was to seize her sister and run, but she knew that one sudden movement would be enough to make Naga strike. She stared at the weaving head with its great hood spread wide, at the flicking blue tongue. Naga's focus was on her sister's face – that's where he would sink his fangs. And once he had bitten, he would hold his teeth deep in her flesh, even if she thrashed about and screamed, as she surely would.

Malini murmured to Banni, 'Do not move so much as an eyelash.' Then she prayed silently to Shiva, reminding Him that Banni Ranawana was a moon child recognised by a sadhu, and pleading for intervention.

Banni stared straight into the eyes of Naga and did not blink.

A shadow passed over the sisters, and over Naga. The shadow skimmed the reeds of the marsh, then returned.

Malini, even as she prayed, glanced up at the sky and saw the shape of a serpent eagle – the only bird in Sri Lanka bold enough to attack Naga. Her heart leapt as the eagle wheeled.

Naga was gone in an instant, slithering into the marsh grass to avoid the talons of his enemy. The eagle did not dive, seeing two humans close to the snake.

149

Within seconds it was high above them again, heading west.

'You are indeed a moon child,' said Malini, and she took her sister in her arms.

Adjuna reappeared on the marsh, bending and straightening as he plunged the long pole into the mud. He raised a hand and waved. The sisters stood on the shore and waited for him to glide the bow of the narrow boat almost to their feet.

'So strange, Sister!' he said. 'As I was returning, a serpent eagle flew overhead! So beautiful.'

When they reached the far shore, Adjuna tied his boat to a jetty. The boys were ecstatic to see them.

Before they parted ways, Malini questioned Adjuna, asking if he knew of a village further west by the name of Ulla Alakana.

'Ulla Alakana, yes,' said Adjuna. 'Two days west.'

'Will we meet soldiers?' said Malini.

'Soldiers, no. Bad people, maybe.'

'Bad people?'

'Bandits who have no gods. They'll kill you for ten rupees.'

'We have lived through worse,' said Malini.

Two days to Ulla Alakana. Malini thought, *Surely the gods intend us to arrive at our destination. Surely we would have perished much sooner if that was to be our fate.*

But she remained wary. She stopped every ten minutes to study the landscape ahead.

They reached a hilly region, and to the south Malini could see a tea plantation where a small number of Tamil women in blue saris were working. Malini had heard on the news that many of the Tamil tea-pickers had abandoned the plantations of North Central Province. This one was not abandoned, but the war had taken its toll. Normally a hundred or more women and girls would be out picking. Most of Sri Lanka's tea plantations were owned by Sinhalese corporations, but the tea-pickers themselves were usually Tamil women. This seemed almost too far north and not high enough for growing tea, so the plantation she could see must have been the last and furthermost from Kandy, many kilometres to the south.

The low hills in the distance were adorned with the white ribbons of narrow waterfalls. From the position of the sun, Malini could see that it would not be necessary to cross those hills. A little further north the land opened into a plateau, and it was beyond that plateau that she would find Ulla Alakana, and her grandfather's farm.

Malini called Banni, Nanda and the boys. 'If we meet with good fortune, we will reach the village in two days,' she said. 'The war has moved east from here. We will be safe.'

She mentioned nothing of bandits. Gayan and Nanda would be alarmed. Amal would probably claim he wanted to find a gun and kill them. When he asked her why she kept stopping to look far ahead, she said, 'To see if rain is coming.'

Although the shortest way to the village in the west was across the centre of the plateau, Malini decided it was safer to skirt the edge of the open land by keeping to the forest fringe.

'Mama! Malini!' Amal called, and everyone stopped. Amal was not as timid as Gayan, but he was still capable of trembling at anything that reminded him of the war. What he'd seen was the tail of an aeroplane, hanging upside down in the forest canopy. All that could be noticed from where they stood was the tail itself and a patch of fuselage. But when Malini came closer, she could see the entire aircraft.

It was a plane without markings of any sort. It was impossible to say which side it belonged to: the SLA soldiers or the Tamil air force. It was empty, a burnt-out shell.

Chattering sparrow-larks gathered above them in the foliage. When they dared, the birds darted down and fed themselves on insects revealed by the moving of the branches. A brown hawk-owl settled in a tree close to the sparrow-larks, waiting to see if a fieldmouse would be spooked into running from the people below. The sparrow-larks, made nervous by the watching owl, set up a great commotion, then flew away altogether.

Malini wondered if the soldiers from the plane had survived. Then she thought about Kandan. She remembered what her father had said to her about those who died while still young and full of strength. 'Heaven makes a space in the air for every person born. When someone dies young, they are torn from the living world and it is years before the space heals over. Sometimes as we walk along, we feel a sudden sadness. Do you know what that is? We have come to a space in the air that is still healing.'

She washed herself in the little stream, dried her face and hands with a towel, closed her eyes for a minute to summon strength, then called Banni, Nanda, Gayan and Amal to start this last stage of the journey to the village of Ulla Alakana. Malini murmured to her appa, far away. 'Appa, it is Malini talking. Your daughters have kept their space in the air. I pray to Lord Shiva that we find you and Amma and that our family will be strong once more.' Then to her mother, her amma. 'I never knew what a burden it is to care for children! I honour your strength, Amma! My children weigh me down.'

The journey west led them through the sparse forest of the plateau where the trees were low and the ground hard. This was not one of the rich agricultural regions of Sri Lanka; no crops would grow in this arid soil. Here and there on the plain, outcrops of stone reared up in strange shapes, as if they had been sculpted by human hand rather than the wind.

They stopped to eat a meal in the shade of one

of these stone monuments. The sun was high and hot and the children were irritable after several hours of walking under that great golden orb. A fight broke out between Amal and Banni over the last mouthful of Pepsi, and then Gayan began a high-pitched shrieking after a moth crawled into his ear. Malini said to Nanda, 'You fix it.' To Banni she said, 'Feed them.' And she sat close by with the maps.

It seemed to Malini that they were now between two highways and were approaching a region of many small villages indicated on the map with square symbols and a number written in Tamil. Ulla Alakana might be any one of those villages. Sooner or later, Malini would have to find someone to ask which village was which. The most urgent landmark to find was what looked on the map to be an important road running north-east to south-west. A number of villages lay along the route of this road, Ulla Alakana among them, maybe.

Nine years had passed since her last visit to her grandfather's farm. There was, at that time, a lull in the civil war and it was possible to drive down the big highway and then along a sealed road and a rough dirt track all the way to the village. She remembered that the village was an oasis of rich greenery in the parched landscape that surrounded it.

The lands of Malini's appappa were beautifully kept. Three natural springs fed an irrigation system that dated back a thousand years or more. Although the village was Tamil, Sinhalese families found a haven there. A small Buddhist temple had been built five hundred years past on the fringe of the orchards that gave the town its living. The temple's ten monks went to the orchards each day and gathered for their needs what fruit was ready, with the full blessing of the Tamil orchardists.

She could not know this, but as Malini sat hunched over the maps, she was being closely watched through the electronic sight of a sniper's rifle. The man who held the rifle had been given the nickname of 'Panaha' some years ago, meaning 'Fifty'. The man was a bounty hunter, and fifty American dollars was the price the government soldiers paid him for a Tamil cadre in uniform. That price was for a dead cadre; for a living one, the price was twenty American dollars. The bounty hunter always took the fifty-dollar option.

From where he lay stretched on the ground with his rifle resting on a tripod, the bounty hunter could, if he chose, kill the girl with one shot. The girl was not a Tiger, but she was the right age, and he could easily dress her body in a tiger-stripe uniform, of which he carried a half-dozen in the panniers of his trail bike. Many girls of her age served with the Tigers. He moved the sight to the others in the group, just out of curiosity, to the two small boys in strange uniforms; to a girl in a green blouse; to another girl in baggy khaki shorts. Who were these idiots? He switched his aim back to the older girl's head and set the sight's red tracking dot to a point just below her left temple. Those with her would scatter once the girl was dead; they would cause no trouble.

For the past little while, Banni had been troubled by a feeling of dread in her heart. She helped Nanda feed the children, but when Nanda handed her a biscuit, she shook her head.

'What's wrong, Banni?'

'Nothing. I don't know.'

'Then eat.'

'Not now.'

Banni went to Malini, bent over the maps.

'We must leave this place,' she said to her sister.

'In a few minutes,' said Malini, paying little attention.

'No, Sister – we must leave now.'

'Don't vex me! I am trying to find the village on these absurd maps! We will leave soon enough.'

Banni walked away with her head bowed. Then she stopped and turned her gaze to the south. She could make out in the distance a place where the low trees grew together more closely. A faint whistling sound hissed in her ears. She moved a little to the right and listened again to the whistling. Then she returned and stood in front of Malini. She said in an urgent whisper. 'Listen to me, Sister. Stay still. Do not move from where you are. Don't speak.'

Malini looked up from the maps with a frown on her face. What now? Had Banni lost her wits after a day in the hot sun? She was about to tell Banni to come to her senses, but something in her sister's stare caused her to remain quiet.

Banni moved closer to her sister. Neither moved a muscle. Banni stood perfectly still, her gaze still fixed on the distant grove of trees.

The bounty hunter paused. A girl had stepped in front of his target. He lifted his sight to her face. She seemed to be staring straight at him, even though he was more than a kilometre away. There was something uncanny in her stare. It was as if she could see him as clearly as he could see her. Everyone around her was motionless, as if carved in stone.

The bounty hunter considered the possibility of first shooting the younger girl, then the older girl. He rested his finger on the trigger with the girl in his sight. He had collected many bounties over the past ten years and would normally have pulled the trigger without further thought. But this time he couldn't. He was a superstitious man who kept good-luck charms in his pockets – the claw of a mother leopard, a Portuguese gold coin from Sri Lanka's distant past, the tooth of a sadhu who had lived to be one hundred and nine years old. The girl's strange stare unnerved him. He heard a whistling sound in his ear, such as an owl makes when it flies overhead in search of its prey.

He said beneath his breath, 'Move yourself, fool. I don't want your blood.'

But the girl remained exactly where she was, staring directly at him.

The bounty hunter, a highly skilled marksman, moved the red dot of his sight to the girl's shoulder. He would shoot to wound her, without killing her, then his second shot would kill the older girl. But as he rested his finger on the trigger, a chill came over him, even in the heat of the high sun. He uttered a string of curses. 'In the name of all the gods, who is this witch?' The girl was still looking at him. For fifty dollars, would he risk a lifetime of bad luck? Would he? He gave the dilemma another sixty seconds' thought, then muttered an oath and unclipped his rifle from the tripod. He packed the weapon away into a cylinder on the back of his trail bike, straddled the saddle, kicked the engine to life and roared away east through the trees. As he rode, he felt in his pocket for his sadhu's tooth, put it to his lips and kissed it. 'I did not kill her,' he said. 'Did you not see? I let her live.'

Banni pointed south towards the sound of the trail bike. A long cloud of dust rose into the air in its wake. Malini, Nanda and the boys watched in silence. Finally, Nanda whispered to Banni, 'Who was it?'

'A bad man,' said Banni. Then to Nanda, 'A biscuit, please.'

Malini studied her sister in wonder. How did she know someone was over there in the trees, so far off? The sadhu had said she was a moon girl, but Malini only half-believed tales of that sort. And yet... No, no. Her sister was just a girl like any other. A little less of a pain than she'd once been, maybe, but still just a girl.

'We'll go now!' Malini called. 'We're looking for a road, a proper black road, not a track. When we find the road, we will ask someone the way to the village. One more day, maybe.'

Chapter 15

The further west they travelled, the more lush the countryside became. The sandy earth of the plateau gave way to rich, rust-coloured soil, and the trees grew taller. Scanning the way ahead, Malini picked out terraced paddy fields on the hillsides, and lower down, thriving market gardens. In this region of Sri Lanka, you could grow anything.

Malini's appappa, Panya Ranawana, had worked for five decades as an actuary in his small town, forever dreaming of the farm his own father had left him at Ulla Alakana. He had told Malini of that dream, more than once. 'When your grandmother, my beloved wife, left this life behind, I knew the time had come, if it was ever to come. It would be my solace, do you see, child? I would grow mangoes, queen pineapples, passionfruit, breadfruit. And if I had success, I would dedicate the happiness it would bring me to your grandmother.' Malini, gazing at the thriving fields in the distance, recalled walking among the fruit trees with her grandfather, and of saying to him, 'You did have success, didn't you, Appappa?'

'Yes, my love. I had success. But when I first came here at the age of sixty, I found a stony waste. It took me ten years to turn it into a jewel. I hired men and women to clear the land of stones.'

It was a story that Malini's grandfather loved to tell. And since she had heard it four or five times, it was her task to ask the right questions at the right moment.

'So many trials you had to face, Appuppa! Isn't that true?'

'So many trials, Malini. So many. Just to bring water to the fields I had to plead with the local authorities for a licence. When I harvested my first crops, I paid the Tamil soldiers to allow my trucks safe passage northwards through land that the Tigers held. And I paid government soldiers to let me send my queen pineapples south to Colombo. Always paying this soldier, paying that soldier! But my fruit was splendid, Malini – splendid! People rushed to buy Ranawana fruit.'

Exhausted though she was, feeling not at all well, Malini slipped into a reverie as she thought of those days with her grandfather. She whispered to herself, *What was your secret, Appappa?* That was what she was expected to ask whenever her grandfather reached this point in his story: 'What was your secret?'

Banni, wondering what on earth her sister was doing, came up beside her and waved her hand in front of Malini's face. 'Hello?' she said. 'Why have we stopped? Why are you talking to yourself?'

161

Malini ignored her, or perhaps didn't even notice her sister. She whispered again, *What was your secret?* And she heard her grandfather's chuckle of pleasure as he prepared to tell her how Ranawana fruit came to be so prized.

'One day, my love, I was looking through the wares in a gypsy peddler's caravan when I came across an old book written by a sadhu in Sanskrit, a language I had taught myself over the years. Page after page advised the reader on every single thing that would improve the growth of fruit. *Fruit is the bounty of heaven,* the sadhu had written. *A peach is a gift to your lips from Lord Shiva. The flesh and juice of every fruit is a message of love. Grow this bounty with reverence.* I took the sadhu's advice. When I planted, I prayed. When I harvested, I gave thanks to every god.'

Banni tugged at her sister's sari. 'Can we go now?' she said.

'Hmm?'

'Can we go now? You're in a trance. It scares me.'

'I was thinking of Appappa,' said Malini, returning to the here and now. 'It would be a shame if I were permitted ten minutes with my thoughts, I suppose. Very well, let's go.'

They walked for a further hour or more, the greenery in the distance gradually coming closer. Malini's strength was ebbing from her body, but she wouldn't allow herself another rest, fearing that if she stopped she would never make her limbs start moving again. Dominating her thoughts was the call she was waiting on from her father. He had said, 'Three days,' and this was the third. She took the phone out of her sari every so often to see if there was a missed call or a message. She would be relieved when they arrived safely at the village, but unless she was reunited with her parents, the journey would mean nothing to her. She desperately needed to hear her father say, 'You have done well, Malini, my beloved,' and to have her mother smother her in kisses and fret over the state of her hair and her fingernails. She wanted to be a child again, or almost a child.

The call came towards evening. But it was not from her father; it was her mother who rang. She was in an emotional state, barely able to talk. She said that she and Malini's father were travelling west towards Ulla Alakana but that Appa had been wounded and could not get to a doctor.

'Wounded?' said Malini. In her anxious state, she felt she was about to faint. 'How?'

'He has been shot! He—'

The call cut out.

Malini dialled the number back. There was no response. She dialled again, then a third and a fourth time.

Half mad with anxiety, she pressed on with the journey, refusing to stop until she came to the paved road just before midnight. She found a concealed place for a camp in the forest near a stream, and saw the children fed and bedded down. Then she dialled her father's mobile number once more.

This time there was an answer. A stranger's voice asked in Sinhala who she was.

'Who am I? Why do you ask? I wish to speak to Chandran Ranawana or Tamara Ranawana.'

The stranger said, 'Again I ask, who are you?'

Malini hesitated briefly before saying that she was the daughter of Chandran Ranawana.

'He is dead,' said the stranger.

'What? No! Please give the phone to my mother!'

She heard another voice in the background, then a third. A new voice, a woman's, said, 'You are the daughter of Chandran Ranawana?'

'Yes! Yes!'

'He is wounded. We are operating.'

'Where are you? Please, I have a right to know!'

'This is a field hospital of Sri Lanka Red Cross.'

'What happened?' Malini asked, but the call cut out.

Malini dialled again, and a further six times without any answer.

There was enough battery left for one call, maybe. Malini saved it in case her mother rang again. She refused to accept what the man had told her. Her father couldn't be dead. It was as the woman had said: he was wounded; he was being operated on; but he was alive.

Malini let the children sleep, but she herself did not sleep at all; she paced up and down, fighting her fear.

At the first light of dawn, she roused the children. She told Banni and Nanda to bathe the boys in the stream and prepare some breakfast. The boys could see how distressed she was and crowded around her, kissing her hands. Banni asked her what news there was of Appa and Amma.

'News? None. Don't ask me.'

Malini had avoided villages for the whole length of the journey, but now she threw caution to the wind and marched alone into the first village she came to on the western side of the paved road. She stopped at a kiosk that sold magazines, peanuts and Coca-Cola. She asked the woman serving in the kiosk the way to the village of Ulla Alakana. The woman, in her middle years but with grey hair escaping from beneath her shawl, asked Malini why she wanted to know.

'Because that's where I am headed, honoured lady,' said Malini.

'Because that is where you are headed,' the woman repeated. 'But why?'

Malini wanted to say, 'That is my business.' But she knew that in a village such as this, anyone's business was everyone's business.

'To find my appappa.'

'What is the name of your grandfather? That is my question.'

'My appappa's name is Panya Ranawana.'

The woman had been sitting. Now she stood and put her hands to her face in surprise. 'I know him!'

'You know my grandfather?'

'A good man! An ornament to our town! He lives alone. His honoured wife died many years ago of a disease called typhus.'

'Your town?'

'I didn't tell you. In these times, it's important to take care. This is the town of Ulla Alakana. Your honoured grandfather is lord of the orchard at the bottom of the hill path. It's an hour's walk.'

Malini took directions from the woman then returned to Banni, Nanda, Amal and Gayan. Tears were running down her face. 'This is the village,' she said. 'This is Ulla Alakana. This is where our appappa lives.'

Banni rushed to her sister and kissed her rapidly on both cheeks. Nanda, Amal and Gayan took their turns to kiss Malini, recognising that she was on the brink of wailing her heart out. 'A happy day,' said Nanda. 'You made this possible, Malini. I think we would have died without you. I think so.'

Gayan made the light clapping sound with his two hands that was his signature of delight. Amal held Malini's hand to his cheek.

Malini dried her eyes on her shawl. 'We walk for twenty minutes on the west side of the paved road. Then we take the dirt road over a hill. Appappa's house is at the bottom of the hill path.'

Is it truly possible? Are we really here? Malini thought. And she began to weep again.

Panya Ranawana employed a housekeeper, a woman of sixty by the name of Varya. She had endured the exhausting life of a tea-picker for many years before finding her present, much more comfortable position. She guarded the peace and the health of Panya Ranawana jealously. Hawkers and peddlers who came to the door were chased away, and she settled any disputes among the orchard workers with a few efficient words. She knew how to count, and with the aid of an electronic calculator she kept track of all the expenses of the orchard. To the orchard workers, fifty of them, Varya was 'Mrs Boss', or sometimes, 'Lady Boss'. She was respected by everyone and admired despite her sharp tongue, for underneath the prickly surface her heart was tender.

Varya had been the housekeeper for the past eight years, so she had not met Malini or Banni. It was for this reason that she watched the approach of the ragtag band of children led by a tall girl in a dirty sari with suspicion. Ripe fruit hung from the trees of the orchard for seven months of the year, and for those seven months, children tried every trick in the book to sneak past the orchard keepers and fill hessians sacks with guavas, passionfruit and apples to sell to peddlers.

Varya hurried out to the gate and called, 'No gypsies, thank you very much! No beggars, either!

Take yourselves somewhere else!'

Malini stepped forward and spoke through the slats of the tall wooden gate. 'Honoured lady, excuse our appearance. I—'

'Your appearance is excused. Now take yourself far away before I call the keepers!'

'Honoured lady, allow me to speak. I—'

'Allow you to speak? You may talk until your face turns blue, but up in the forest, not here. Now make haste out of my sight!'

'I am Malini Ranawana. I am the granddaughter of Panya Ranawana. This is my sister, Banni. Please, honoured lady, inform my grandfather that we are at the gate.'

Varya, about to shout for the keepers, suddenly froze. She looked at the tall girl more closely. And in her mind she compared the girl she saw before her with the girl in the photograph that Panya Ranawana kept on the wooden mantelpiece in his living room, next to pictures of his son and daughter-in-law and younger granddaughter. This girl was older than the Malini in the picture, and much dirtier, but...was it possible?

'You say you are my honoured master's granddaughter? What is your father's name? And your mother's name?'

Malini said, 'My appa is Chandran Ranawana. My amma is Tamara.'

Varya's hands flew to her face. 'All the gods! Malini, is it you?'

She took a ring of keys she wore on a belt around her waist and quickly unlocked the gate. 'And this one is Banni, the beauty? Come in, come in!'

She embraced Malini, then Banni, and showed the whole party into the house, calling to her master. 'Honoured sir! Come and see! Honoured sir! By a miracle – your granddaughters!'

Panya Ranawana, awakened from his afternoon nap by the noise, made all the haste he could on his ancient legs.

Varya called, 'In the kitchen, honoured sir!'

Panya stopped in the kitchen doorway and gazed at the small crowd of children gathered around the table.

'Malini, my beloved child! Banni, the beauty! All the gods, what a day for this frail old man! Let me hold you.'

Malini and Banni hugged their appappa and kissed his hands.

'Children,' said Panya Ranawana, 'ten thousand prayers have been answered! My son and his honoured wife? Do not give me news my heart cannot bear!'

Malini told her grandfather that his son, her father, was wounded but in the care of the Red Cross with her mother. More she could not say.

Banni let out a yelp of alarm. 'You did not tell me this!' she said.

'I could not,' said Malini. 'Forgive me, Banni.'

Malini introduced Nanda, Amal and Gayan, each of them suddenly shy in the house of Malini's grandfather. Nanda said, 'Pleased to meet you, sir,' and Amal and

Gayan repeated her words, struggling to master Tamil.

Malini gave a brief account of the long journey from the coast. Then she asked for a glass of water.

Varya hurried to the stone water jar and filled a tall glass, but before Malini could so much as sip, she fainted and crumpled to the wooden floor.

Chapter 16

A fever raged in Malini like a typhoon that roars in from the sea and turns the world upside down. She did not know where she was or who she was. She saw a house on fire, flames hurling themselves into a crimson sky. She saw a demon with a hundred heads pulling birds from the air and swallowing them whole. She saw a funeral pyre with a body on top, and the body was that of a girl, and many people stood close by and wept and sang songs of mourning.

She said, 'It is me. I am leaving this world.'

A cup was held to her lips. Water ran down her throat. Then the water stopped and the fire returned.

She heard a voice, that of a man. He said, 'It is the return of malaria. This can happen. She has exhausted her body, and malaria has returned.'

A long time passed, so it seemed. Malini in her fevered state said, 'I am ready to die.' She saw Kandan as he'd looked in life, but graver, no smile, just a sadness in his eyes.

On the funeral pyre the body caught fire and burned like a torch.

She saw a mansion of white stone. She walked a long path lined with trees and climbed fifty steps to a pool of silver water. Tall doors swung open. She walked through a hall where guests were eating from a banquet table. Someone said, 'Her eyelids moved!' An old man with wrinkled hands held her face. He said, 'I bless all the gods! This child lives!'

Ten days into the fever, Malini's appa and amma arrived at the orchard in a rusty yellow utility purchased with the American dollars Chandran Ranawana had kept hidden in the soles of his boots. Chandran was bleeding through bandages around his chest. He had been shot five times by government soldiers who had been ordered to kill Tamil men fleeing the enclaves on the coast. The soldiers had lined up more than a hundred Tamils – not only men but young women they suspected of having fought for the LTTE – and fired at them. The soldiers had left the bodies where they lay. Relatives of the murdered men, concealed in the forest, rushed to the site of the killings as soon as the soldiers departed. Malini's mother found her kanavar badly wounded but alive. With the help of other Tamils, she carried him for two days to a Red Cross field hospital, where his life was saved. Two weeks later came the purchase of the yellow utility, and the journey by night to Ulla Alakana.

A woman with tears in her eyes was bathing Malini. She held a blue cloth. She dipped the cloth into a brass bowl and ran it over Malini's bare arms, over her legs.

Malini said to the woman, 'Who are you to wash my body in this way?'

The woman said, 'Your amma, child.'

She said to the woman, 'My amma has left the earth. Don't tell me lies. Whoever lies to me, I will kill.'

The woman dried Malini's body then dressed her tenderly in white cotton. Malini said to the woman, 'Bring me my sword.'

Time was a flock of white birds gliding across a sky of blue and red. Then it was a stream. She knelt and put her hand into the stream. A blue fish with golden eyes leapt into her arms. The fish shed its tail and became a blue cloth. The woman returned and was again bathing her body. She said to the woman, 'Bring me my sword, demon!'

The woman kissed her on her cheeks and on her forehead and at last on her lips.

A morning came when Malini woke and knew in an instant who she was and where she was. Her sister, Banni, was sleeping in an armchair beside the bed. Banni was dressed not in jeans and her pink shirt but in a blue sari. She looked so much older! On a table close to the bed sat an assortment of medicine bottles. One was half full of pink liquid. Malini could read the

English script on the label: *Do not employ when allergies are suspected.*

Malini said, 'Sister…'

Banni's eyes opened slowly. She gazed at Malini.

Malini said again, 'Sister…'

Banni sat bolt upright. She sprang from the armchair and fell to kissing Malini rapidly all over her face. 'I bless all the gods! I bless Shiva a million times!'

Then Banni called, 'Amma! Appa!'

A minute passed. Malini's father hurried into the room, and her mother. Her father's shirt was open and bandages circled his chest.

Malini lifted her arms and closed them around her father's neck. When he raised his face and gazed at her, his eyes were glittering with tears.

He said, 'Blessed girl, I said a thousand times you would live! A thousand times I said it. *This girl will live. This girl with a lion's heart, she will live!*'

Malini's mother sat on the other side of the bed. She held Malini's hand against her heart. 'You said so, Husband, a thousand times.'

Malini could see Banni over her father's shoulder – Banni, who was so much older in her blue sari. Her face was soaked in tears. She murmured over and over, 'Sister…Sister…Sister…'

Nanda and the boys ran into the room. Nanda took Malini's hand. Amal and Gayan clamoured to get to her, but were held back by Nanda. Amal shouted at the top of his voice, 'I will destroy any who stop me!' Malini laughed for perhaps two seconds, then the

174

laughter turned to tears. She felt that the happiness that surged through her so strongly could almost kill her with its force.

Almost three weeks had passed since Malini had stood at the gate and announced that she was the granddaughter of Panya Ranawana. In that time, she had twice been thought in the bower of Shiva, and twice she had moved her eyelids and restored hope to the hearts of those watching. The doctor had said, 'The girl intends to live, so it seems.'

The doctor was guessing in part when he said that Malini's fever was a new bout of malaria. What he did know was that Malini had been dangerously fatigued before she became ill. With the country in the state it was after the war, it was impossible to have Malini taken to a hospital in Colombo. Everything was chaotic. Tamils were being turned away from clinics and hospitals. Many thousands had died in the past month. The fighting had ended all over Sri Lanka, but murder had not.

If the idea of 'innocent civilians' had ever meant much in warfare, it meant even less now that the civil war was truly ending. The 'human shields' – Tamil civilians, held by the LTTE cadres – died in far greater numbers than LTTE soldiers when the government troops attacked the enclaves.

The news of these deaths in the thousands came through on the BBC World Service. Malini and her father, still recovering from what should have killed them, listened together for two weeks to the news, then by mutual agreement, gave up their sorrowful vigil beside the radio in Panya's living room. Instead, they walked in the orchard for hours each day, stopping to watch the birds falling from the air onto the ripe guavas. The keepers chased them away by beating drums and shouting at the tops of their voices. 'Ho, thieves! Fly or die, thieves!'

Malini and her father regained their strength over the next two months. With the village school shut down in this post-war period of chaos, Malini made her grandfather's living room a classroom and taught Amal, Gayan, Banni and any children of the village who cared to attend. Her subjects were mathematics, science, geography, history, Tamil, Sinhala and English. The children sat on the floor with notebooks and pens while Malini moved from one group to another encouraging and correcting. She had a knack for teaching and before long had a school of seventeen, Tamil and Sinhalese, aged from four to thirteen. As for her own studies, she kept up with maths at an online university and read her grandfather's English novels and poetry.

For the broken society outside the classroom, there was nothing she could do. Remaking a country is too big a task for one person, or even for a thousand. It is a task for millions. One thing that could be achieved, though, was to remember Kandan in some special way. Prayers were offered at the shrine of Shiva in the orchard each day for eight days, but it was Gayan who one morning came running into the house holding a small mango tree in a cardboard planter. It had become Gayan's habit to help the orchard workers plant new trees in the western section of the orchard, and this morning an idea had leapt into his head.

He stood panting before Panya, holding the tree above his head with both hands. 'Kandan!' he said. Panya, was baffled. He thought the boy had lost his wits. He called for Nanda. When she came, Gayan said, in a state of high excitement, 'For Kandan! This tree!'

And so it was that a mango tree was planted in the west of the orchard to commemorate Kandan's life. Malini and Banni, Nanda, Amal, Panya, Chandran Ranawana and his wife Tamara, Varya and three orchard workers watched on as Gayan lifted the small tree from its cardboard planter and lowered it into a hole. He patted the soil flat around the base of the tree, then stood upright and tapped his hands together in his particular way. He said, 'This is for our friend Kandan.'

Malini said, 'For our friend Kandan.'

Then all of those watching said, 'For Kandan.'

One morning when all the children of her school were working away in four separate groups, and Banni in her sari was bent over her maths questions with a frown of concentration on her face, a blessed moment came Malini's way. The weather was not too hot, and the ceiling fan was purring softly. In the kitchen she could hear her father, her mother, Varya and her grandfather quietly discussing the business of the orchard, since it was agreed that Malini's father would help with the management of the estate until it was safe to return to their village on the coast. Nanda, at last putting on a little weight, was sewing a rag doll as a present for a girl from the village, an exquisite thing with small buttons for eyes and blue wool for hair. From outside came the cries of the orchard workers as they scaled their ladders beneath the guava boughs. Malini stood still at the centre of this small, thriving world and drank in happiness, gladness and gratitude. She thought, *It is something to still be here, my heart beating, everyone absorbed in tasks other than survival. It is something.*

Her father walked into the living room that was now a classroom and looked across at his daughter. She looked at him, at her father, and smiled.

Each understood the happiness in the heart of the other.

Author's Note

I first visited Colombo, the capital city of Sri Lanka, when I was a kid of sixteen, travelling the world in search of adventure. The country at that time was known as Ceylon. From the deck of the ship, the city looked like the most thrilling destination on earth. The sun was setting and the whitewashed buildings of Ceylon's colonial era turned a bright orange, then a more subdued pink. Dozens of small wooden craft crowded around the ship, each boat packed with fruit and fabrics for sale to the westerners gazing down from the deck. The vendors sang songs celebrating their wares, and called out to the tourists above. 'Many fine mangoes for you, sirs and ladies! Pineapples so tasty, indeed!' The noise the vendors made was like an orchestra of voices, the music rising and falling. At that time, the island was at peace. I thought, *Such a beautiful land*.

When I next visited Sri Lanka in 2005, peace was the last thing that came to mind. The shocking violence of a civil war that had been raging since 1983 had left a dark cloud of suspicion and resentment hovering over the island. There was still great beauty to be seen in this vivid green land, but wherever I went, I met people who were sorrowing for what had become of Sri Lanka's civil society, and sorrowing, too, for sons and daughters, husbands and wives killed in the fighting. At that time, a truce had been proposed, but I did not meet anyone, Tamil or Sinhalese, who believed for a moment that the war would soon be over. I came across raw hatred and I heard angry denunciations, but more often I encountered sadness and regret.

The war in Sri Lanka pitted Sinhalese against Tamils, the two major ethnic groups of the island. In 2014, the overwhelming majority of Sri Lankans are Sinhalese (around seventy-four per cent), and largely follow the Buddhist faith. The Tamil people, including immigrant Tamils from southern India, make up approximately fifteen per cent of the island's population, and follow the Hindu faith, for the most part. Both Sinhalese and Tamils have inhabited the island for millenia. The age-old Tamil population was joined by some hundreds of thousands of Tamils from southern India in the nineteenth century. These 'newcomers' were recruited by the colonial British to work in tea plantations.

The Tamil population tends to be concentrated in the north of the island, and along the east coast. Like minorities in other lands, the Tamils feel more secure living close to each other, forming communities where the Tamil religion and culture dominate. But wherever people live as a minority in their homeland, such security can often feel under threat. After Sri Lanka achieved independence from Britain in 1948, the Tamils of the island felt increasingly marginalised by a government dominated by the Sinhalese. Tamils claimed that a whole range of government policies were designed to restrict their access to education, to employment in the public service and to the securing of finance for businesses. In 1956, the Tamil language itself ceased to be recognised as an official state language. In the 1970s, militant Tamil groups emerged to carry the fight for equality beyond peaceful protests. The dominating figure in Tamil politics was Velupillai Prabhakaran, who would one day lead the Liberation Tigers of Tamil Eelam (LTTE) in an armed struggle to establish a Tamil state in the north of the island.

It might have been predicted as early as a decade after independence that civil war would break out in Sri Lanka, given the grievances of the Tamil people and the mounting impatience with their political claims among the majority Sinhalese. But I doubt that anyone at that time would have foreseen the extraordinary brutality of the war. For this was one of the most savage conflicts fought since the end of the Second World War in 1945. Although the war is usually considered to be three wars, with truces in between outbreaks, each stage of the conflict was equally violent and bloody. Terrible war crimes and atrocities were committed by both sides in the conflict, including the massacre of civilians, torture, and the destruction of entire villages. Further killings were carried out by bandit groups. Unarmed civilians were considered no different to armed combatants. Children were killed in great numbers. And this was the war in which the world first heard of 'suicide bombing': human beings, strapped with explosives, blowing themselves up in crowded areas.

The armed forces of the Sri Lankan government gradually gained the upper hand over the LTTE from 2006 onwards. The LTTE surrendered in May 2009 after a series of terrible defeats. In the final months of the war, Tamil civilians in great numbers became trapped in enclaves in the north and east of the island and many died during the final assaults of the Sri Lankan Army. Human rights groups had been calling for an international investigation of war crimes over the entire period of the civil war, and have recently succeeded in having the United Nations Human Rights Council agree to an enquiry.

Today, many thousands of Tamils remain displaced within Sri Lanka, and a number of the issues of discrimination against Tamils that led to the civil war still persist. I recall particularly two comments from my last visit to the island in 2005. The first is that of a young man I questioned about his views on the war. He said, 'Tamils do not belong in Sri Lanka. India is their home. They should leave.' The second is the voice of a much older man, a shop owner in Colombo. 'Robert, what can I say to you about this war? I can say this: heaven forgive all of us. All.'

I have written about wars and the refugees they create in a number of books, but I hadn't written about Sri Lanka until the opportunity came to tell the fictional story of Malini. I wanted to show, in the character of Malini, that courage is not something we either have or don't have, but something that may come to life in our hearts just when the need is greatest.

Timeline

1815 Ceylon becomes a British Crown colony. Tamil plantation workers arrive from India.

1948 British Ceylon gains independent Dominion status. D.S. Senanayake becomes first prime minister.

1956 Prime Minister S.W.R.D. Bandaranaike elected on wave of Sinhalese political nationalism. Sinhala Only Act denies official recognition of the Tamil language and increases tension between majority, Buddhist Sinhalese and minority, Muslim Tamils. More than 100 Tamils killed in violent protests.

1958 Anti-Tamil riots leave estimated 200 people dead and thousands of Tamils displaced.

1960–1965 Sirimavo Bandaranaike, the world's first female prime minister, governs Ceylon.

1970 Sirimavo Bandaranaike returns to power and extends nationalisation program. Ethnic riots continue as official discrimination against Tamils escalates.

1972 Ceylon becomes Republic of Sri Lanka with Buddhism as the official religion, further antagonising Tamil minority.

1976 Liberation Tigers of Tamil Eelam (LTTE), also known as Tamil Tigers, forms with Velupillai Prabhakaran as military commander. LTTE demands a separate state in Tamil-dominated areas of the north and east.

1981 Sinhalese policemen accused of burning Jaffna library containing over 97 000 books and manuscripts – a major turning point in ethnic riots. Tamils demand government protection for cultural heritage.

1983 First Eelam War. Civil War erupts when LTTE ambush Sri Lankan Army (SLA) checkpoint on Jaffna Peninsula killing 13 government soldiers and sparking 'Black July' anti-Tamil riots in Colombo and elsewhere. Estimated 3000 people dead. Many thousands of Tamils flee abroad.

1985 LTTE control Jaffna and most of Jaffna Peninsula.

1987 SLA launches 'Operation Liberation' to secure Jaffna Peninsula. Indo–Sri Lanka Peace Accord grants concessions to Tamils. Tamil becomes an official language. Indian troops begin 'peacekeeping' operations in north-eastern Sri Lanka but are quickly enmeshed in three-year war with LTTE.

1989 Ranasinghe Premadasa assumes presidency and requests Indian troops leave.

1990 Second Eelam War. Indian troops withdraw. Violence between SLA and LTTE escalates in Eastern Province. SLA attempts to retake Jaffna. LTTE controls large areas of northern Sri Lanka and expels thousands of Muslims from Jaffna.

1991 Estimated 5000 LTTE cadres surround SLA's Elephant Pass military base. More than 2000 killed. Government forces fail to retake Jaffna. Suspected LTTE suicide bomber assassinates Indian Prime Minister Rajiv Gandhi.

1992 LTTE destroys Palliyathidal village. An estimated 240 people killed in one of the worst massacres of the civil war.

1993 President Ranasinghe Premadasa killed in LTTE bomb attack.

1995 Third Eelam War. LTTE sinks naval craft. Jaffna falls to government forces. LTTE sets up new 'capital' in Kilinochchi and compels more than 350 000 civilians to flee to Vanni region.

1996–1999 Civil war rages across north and east of Sri Lanka: 200 000 civilians flee violence. LTTE launches 'Operation Unceasing Waves' and wins the Battle of Mullaitivu. LTTE bombings increase with loss of many civilian lives, including bombing of Sri Lanka's holiest Buddhist site, the Temple of Tooth.

1999–2001 LTTE presses towards Jaffna, cuts all SLA supply lines and captures Elephant Pass military base. Human rights groups estimate more than one million internally displaced persons.

2002 Sri Lankan government and LTTE sign Norwegian-mediated ceasefire. Decommissioning of weapons begins. Jaffna Peninsula road reopens. Government lifts economic embargoes on LTTE who drop demand for separate state.

2003 LTTE pulls out of peace talks, but ceasefire holds.

2004 Tsunami devastates Sri Lankan coastal communities. More than 30 000 people killed, 2.5 million left homeless. Mahinda Rajapaksa elected president. State of emergency declared after suspected LTTE assassin kills foreign minister Lakshman Kadirgamar.

2006–7 LTTE and government forces resume fighting in north-east in worst clashes since 2002 ceasefire. Government steadily drives LTTE out of eastern strongholds. Peace talks fail in Geneva.

2008 President Rajapaksa pulls out of ceasefire agreement and launches massive offensive against LTTE, progressively retaking critical LTTE strongholds in Vanni heartland.

2009 January–April SLA captures Kilinochchi and most of Jaffna Peninsula. LTTE's new base at Mullaitivu also falls. Increasing brutality from both sides results in mounting civilian casualties. Sri Lankan military sets up 'no-fire zones' for civilians in Mullaitivu district. An estimated 350 000 civilians end up trapped in ever-shrinking 14-square-kilometre zone. Sri Lankan government rejects United Nations (UN) call for ceasefire and accuses LTTE of using civilians as human shields. UN estimates 6500 civilians killed and 14 000 wounded. More than 100 000 internally displaced persons in camps in Vavuniya, Jaffna, Mannar and Trincomalee. UN High Commissioner for Human Rights accuses both sides of war crimes.

May Estimated 15 000–20 000 dead in final four months of civil war. UN describes fighting as a 'bloodbath' for civilians. SLA captures last LTTE-held section of coastline, retakes Kilinochchi and declares victory. Velupillai Prabhakaran killed in final battle. Estimated 70 000 civil-war related deaths and hundreds of thousands more displaced by conflict.

2010 Sri Lanka holds first presidential elections in twenty years amid international allegations of war crimes. President Mahinda Rajapaksa re-elected.

2012 Estimated 370 000 internally displaced persons in Sri Lanka.

2013 United Nations Human Rights Council (UNHRC) passes resolution urging Sri Lanka to conduct independent investigation into alleged war crimes.

2014 UNHRC votes to open international investigation into possible war crimes by both Sri Lankan government and LTTE in final stages of civil war.

Glossary

Sinhala

aetta-da? is it true?

boru-da? is it false?

dhura far away

naeh no

namgi sister

oba dhanagana lakema sathutak pleased to meet you

oba kohendha? where are you from?

sadarayen piligannawa you are welcome

sohoyura brother

Tamil

amma mother

appa father

appappa grandfather

ayya used to address elder men

ennai thodaathe! don't touch me!

eppadi irukkinka? how are you?

Kadavul kapatra vendum God save us

kalai vanakkam good morning

kalaiyil in the morning

kanavar husband

mannikkanum sorry

manniththu vidunggal   excuse me

meen   fish

nee ennai yemathikitu!   you're cheating me!

ora nimidam!   one moment!

pachadi   savoury Tamil dish of grated vegetable, tamarind, shallots, ginger and mustard seeds

pattu vetty   traditional Tamil costume for men; long silk cloth worn like a sarong and tied at the waist

pottu   a dot worn on the forehead and commonly known as a bindi in North India

sadhu   holy man

thayavuseithu   please

vadai   savoury fritter with a crunchy shell, made from rice flour, lentils and chilies

Find out more about...

Sri Lanka

http://www.britannica.com/EBchecked/topic/561906/
Sri-Lanka

http://www.globaleducation.edu.au/2384.html

http://www.infolanka.com/photo/

Hoffmann, Sara E. *Sri Lanka in Pictures*, Twenty-First Century Books, Minneapolis, 2006

Conflict in Sri Lanka

http://www.insightonconflict.org/conflicts/sri-lanka/
conflict-profile/#52

http://www.theguardian.com/world/2009/may/18/
sri-lanka-conflict

Children and Sri Lankan conflict

http://www.irinnews.org/report/82991/sri-lanka-
children-suffering-the-most-in-conflict-unicef

http://www.irinnews.org/report/82529/
sri-lanka-unicef-urges-tigers-to-ensure-free-
movement-out-of-conflict-areas

http://www.unicef.org/infobycountry/sri_lanka_41670.
html

Walters, Eric & Adrian Bradbury, *When Elephants Fight: The Lives of Children in Conflict in Afghanistan, Bosnia, Sri Lanka, Sudan and Uganda*, Orca Book Publishers, Victoria, 2008

Liberation Tigers of Tamil Eelam

http://edition.cnn.com/2009/WORLD/asiapcf/05/18/sri.lanka.conflict.explainer/index.html?iref=24hours

Child soldiers in Sri Lanka

http://www.unicef.org/infobycountry/sri_lanka_48286.html

https://www.youtube.com/watch?v=sOA0IjVL_NU

Acknowledgements

My thanks to Varuni Kanagasundaram for her assistance with the translation of various terms employed in the text.

I also want to thank Lyn White for her great vision in fashioning the series of books of which *Malini* is a part, and Sophie Splatt for her extraordinary commitment as editor.

Publisher's note

The publisher would like to thank Nadesan Sundaresan for his assistance with Tamil terms used in the book.

The publisher would also like to note that the towns of Ankapur, Satham and Ulla Alakana are fictional.

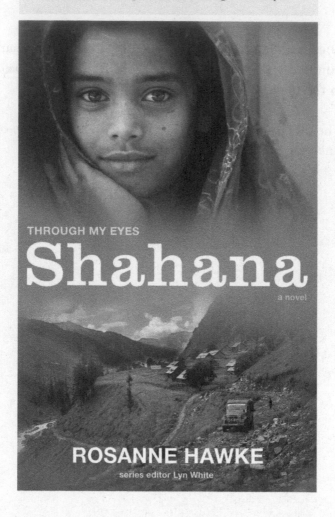

THROUGH MY EYES

Amina

a novel

J. L. POWERS

series editor Lyn White

A moving story of one child's
life in the conflict zone of
Mogadishu, Somalia.

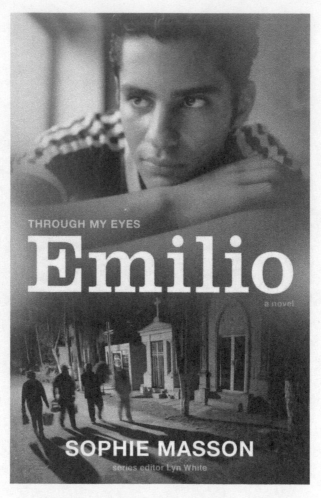

THROUGH MY EYES

Emilio

a novel

SOPHIE MASSON

series editor Lyn White

A suspenseful story of one child's experience of the drug wars in Mexico.